"You think I might be in danger?" Lydia asked.

Jesse kept his gaze on the road as he drove her home. "I hope not, but it's a possibility if the bomber thinks you can ID him."

"I can't. Yet. But what if I did see him and I can't remember?"

"You suffered a head trauma," he reminded her. "Not remembering, especially right away, isn't uncommon. Don't force yourself."

"Are you sure you work for the police? I would have thought you'd have wanted me to remember right now."

"I know you. Force won't work." He threw her half a grin.

"I've been trying, and I can remember a few bits, like how I felt when I heard the laugh track. After that, nothing much else. Lunch was starting," she said, shifting toward him. "I just thought of that."

He glanced at her smile, which lit her whole face. "See? It will come."

Jesse pulled into her driveway, the same house he had picked her up at as a teenager. A memory flashed into his mind—of eons ago when he was a different person.

Margaret Daley, an award-winning author of ninety books (five million sold worldwide), has been married for over forty years and is a firm believer in romance and love. When she isn't traveling, she's writing love stories, often with a suspense thread, and corralling her three cats, who think they rule her household. To find out more about Margaret, visit her website at margaretdaley.com.

Books by Margaret Daley

Love Inspired Suspense

Alaskan Search and Rescue

The Yuletide Rescue
To Save Her Child
The Protector's Mission

Capitol K-9 Unit

Security Breach

Guardians, Inc.

Christmas Bodyguard
Protecting Her Own
Hidden in the Everglades
Christmas Stalking
Guarding the Witness
Bodyguard Reunion

Visit the Author Profile page at Harlequin.com for more titles.

THE PROTECTOR'S MISSION

MARGARET DALEY

HARLEQUIN® LOVE INSPIRED® SUSPENSE

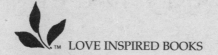

Recycling programs
for this product may
not exist in your area.

LOVE INSPIRED BOOKS

ISBN-13: 978-0-373-44690-2

The Protector's Mission

Copyright © 2015 by Margaret Daley

www.Harlequin.com

Printed in U.S.A.

God is our refuge and strength,
a very present help in trouble.
—Psalms 46:1

To Mike, Shaun, Abbey and Aubrey

ONE

Lydia McKenzie swung open the door to Melinda's Bistro and plowed right into a middle-aged man wearing a navy blue hoodie that shrouded his gray eyes and the scar slashing his cheek. "Sorry."

The guy, holding one of the restaurant take-out sacks, mumbled something and scurried away.

Lydia spied Bree Stone, a doctor and friend from childhood, and headed toward her table. "Sorry I'm late. Had an emergency at work. I hope you got my text." After several hours in surgery at the veterinary hospital, Lydia finally eased into a chair and relaxed.

"I certainly know what an emergency is. We're a doctor short at the hospital, so I'm taking an extra shift to fill in." Bree gathered her purse and put money on the table to pay her tab. "What kind of emergency?"

"It involved one of the rescue dogs from the bombing at the church. A police K-9." Right now she could use a neck and shoulder massage. Pain radiated down her back. "A few days ago, I tended to two rescue dogs that had been injured while searching for survivors at the church, but one of them took a turn for the worse this morning. I had to remove his left hind leg in order to save him. The decision broke my heart because it ends his career, but he'll live."

Bree started to rise but sat back down. "Jesse Hunt's Brutus?"

The mention of Jesse made Lydia's breath catch. She tried to avoid seeing him as much as possible, which was hard since she worked with Northern Frontier Search and Rescue and went to SAR sites to be there if a dog needed medical help. Jesse was often there with his Rottweiler. "No, Officer Nichols with the Anchorage K-9 Unit. He sometimes works with your husband at search and rescue sites."

"Yes, Nichols was brought into the ER last Friday. David was upset. He came to the hospital as soon as he could to see how he was."

"How's he doing?" Lydia shook the image of Jesse Hunt, once a friend, from her mind. When she returned to Anchorage last year, she renewed several friendships, but not with Jesse, whom she'd betrayed right after she'd graduated from high school.

"He's still on the critical list. His accident shows me how dangerous my husband's job is, but David wouldn't do anything else." Bree rose. "I wish I could stay. But I have to be in early because the other doctor is sick."

"We'll catch up later." Lydia rolled her shoulders and released a long breath.

Bree smiled. "When we both slow down. Tell Kate hi for me. She's been asking me about being a doctor."

"She has?" She should know that, but she and her seventeen-year-old sister had clashed a lot since she'd become her guardian last year.

"Yes, she doesn't think she can work with animals

like you and your dad, but she's interested in the medical field. See you."

Lydia watched Bree weave through the tables starting to fill up with people coming in for an early lunch. She scanned the bistro, trying to decide whether to stay and eat or order and take it back to the Aurora Animal Hospital down the street, the veterinary practice she inherited from her father when he died last year. They treated large and small animals as well as the Northern Frontier SAR dogs and the K-9s that worked with the police.

Her gaze settled on Melinda, the owner of the restaurant, talking to a man with dark brown hair sticking out of a black ball cap. The guy took Melinda's hand and moved closer. Was this Todd, the boyfriend she'd been telling Lydia about this past month?

Lydia started to look away to give them some privacy when she spied the man lean toward Melinda, a furious expression on his face. Melinda jerked her hand from his grasp, and the guy pivoted and stormed away, passing Lydia's table.

She averted her look toward a man and a young woman sitting at the table next to her. She knew the guy. He worked at the drugstore—

"Sorry you saw that, Lydia."

She looked up at Melinda. "I'm the one sorry for staring. Are you all right?"

The bistro owner waved her hand. "Boyfriend problems. He isn't too happy with me at the moment." Melinda slipped into the chair next to Lydia. "How have you been?"

"Tired. I had to operate on one of the K-9 dogs that

was hurt at the church bomb site. It's been all over the news."

"That's what everyone's been talking about. Two bombings close together."

Lydia shivered when she thought about the pictures she'd seen on the news. "I know some police officers, and they're working overtime."

"Yeah, I heard there's no connection between the hardware store and the church, but they were only ten days apart. Do you think it's the same person? Have you heard if it's the same MO?"

"It sounds like it. Both times there was a laugh track that sounded seconds before the bomb went off."

"What a sick person!" Melinda rose. "Are you going to eat lunch here or order takeout since Bree left?"

"Takeout. The veggie wrap."

"It shouldn't take too long." Melinda headed for the kitchen in the back.

Glad to be sitting for a few minutes, Lydia glanced at the different people coming into the bistro. Some she recognized because they were regulars, like herself, but a couple were new to her—a young, petite woman with an older gentleman, a young man with long brown hair and a bald man about thirty-five or forty. She loved to people watch. She'd once considered being a writer, but her love of animals clinched her decision to be a vet and follow in her father's footsteps. She'd hoped that decision would reconcile them. It hadn't.

Before Melinda brought her takeout, she made her way down a long hallway to the restroom. A man slipped out the exit door at the end of the corridor. Odd, it wasn't used much.

A few minutes later as she came out of the woman's

bathroom and paused, she panned the dining area, pleased to see the restaurant doing so well. But one of the new customers had left. Maybe the bistro didn't serve what he wanted. She noticed Melinda carrying a takeout bag toward the table where she'd been sitting.

But before Lydia moved forward, a blast of maniacal-sounding laughter resonated through the restaurant. Melinda dropped the sack, a look of horror on her face. Lydia took only two steps back into the hallway before her world exploded.

Sergeant Jesse Hunt took Brutus out of the back of his SUV, secured his leash and walked toward the rubble of the church he attended. One person still remained missing and two were found dead in the bombing last Wednesday. He was on duty and had only stopped by to see David Stone, the head of Northern Frontier SAR, at the bombing site to assess it after the two people were hurt searching it Friday.

"Have they stabilized the structure?" Jesse asked as he approached David.

His friend turned toward him, a grim expression on his face. "Yes, this morning. At least this time I hope nothing else happens. I don't want any more people hurt, but we need to check thoroughly for the one missing."

"Yeah, I've seen people found days later and I heard of someone who lasted a week in the wreckage. That's why I'm here. I can help later after my shift."

"Good. It's nice that late August still gives us long days."

"Is Pastor Paul around?"

"No, he went to a parishioner's house. They're making plans for holding a church service here on Sunday."

"That sounds like him. Someone bombing his church isn't going to stop him from having worship services." Jesse surveyed the large mounds of debris, noting some were marked already searched. His church had been large and thriving. At first the authorities wondered if it had been a crime associated with religion, but as they investigated they discovered too many links to the hardware store destroyed a week and a half before the church. The establishments weren't connected, but the way the bombings were carried out indicated the same person or persons did both, down to the type of bomb, detonated with a timer and the sound of a laugh track.

"At the hardware store there weren't any deaths or injuries, but you and I know the two who died here."

"And the one missing." Jesse's cell phone rang. As he answered the call, he saw it was his commander. "Hunt here."

"There's been a third bombing at Melinda's Bistro, down the street from the Aurora Animal Hospital."

"I know the place. Brutus and I are on our way." Jesse hung up as David received a call, no doubt about the new bombing.

Jesse waved at David, then jogged with Brutus toward his SUV. Settled in his car, he switched on his engine and sirens. Fifteen minutes later he parked his car with other police cruisers and hurried toward the crime scene. The whole street was blocked off. So far, if this was the same MO, there had been only one bomb going off, but this bomber was escalating with each site, the amount of time between each bombing and from the look of the site the size of the bomb. Melinda's Bistro would have just started serving lunch, which meant probably more deaths than the previous one. Did the killer take it even further with the addition of another bomb?

When he arrived at the command post, he assessed the destruction up close. A shudder snaked through him. A cloud of dust hung in the still air where the restaurant had once been, a two-story building brought to the ground, except for one small area where the top floor remained, but heavily damaged. Cries floated to him, some from within the massive debris of concrete, wood and brick.

His gut knotted, and his determination to catch the perpetrator intensified. He'd ask Thomas Caldwell, the detective overseeing the first two bombings, if he could be on the task force the department was forming. He searched the police officers, found his longtime friend and headed straight for him.

"When can we start searching for survivors?" Jesse asked. The site had to be stabilized first to protect everyone, including the survivors.

Thomas shifted his attention to Jesse, his shoulders slumped as though he'd been up forty-eight hours, which was possible. A scowl carved deep lines into Thomas's face. "As soon as we get the okay that it's safe. Until then I could use you and Brutus to check for any other bombs in the area."

"Will do, and I want on the task force you're heading."

"I already put your name down. You were at the top of the list. I have two other K-9 officers searching this side of the street. One that way. The other opposite." Thomas pointed toward the buildings flanking Melinda's Bistro. "But if the bomber is getting more violent, it won't be long before we start seeing multiple bombs. All the shops have been evacuated, necessary personnel only, so be on the lookout for looters."

Jesse started at one end of the street and investigated anything that remotely looked suspicious. Most of the buildings' windows were blown out, and the structures suffered minor damage. He was acquainted with Melinda and most likely she had been in her bistro. Would there be any survivors? From what was left of the restaurant, he didn't have high hopes for anyone, even after hearing the faint cries.

At the other end of the street, he saw Bree Stone admitted into the blocked off area. She had some medical personnel with her. He detoured to meet her in the middle of the street. "Are you setting up a medical tent?"

"Yes. Have you heard of any survivors? I haven't been told anything."

"They're stabilizing the site and making sure there aren't any other bombs. As you can tell, it's pretty chaotic."

"David is coming."

"I know. I was with him when we both got the call."

Bree chewed on her bottom lip. "I was in that restaurant ten minutes before the bomb went off. I had to get back to work, but one of my friends was still there."

"Have you checked to see where she is?"

"Yes, and she hasn't returned to the animal hospi-" Bree studied him. "You two dated in high school, remember correctly. Lydia McKenzie."

Lydia McKenzie. Jesse could feel the color drain his face. His heartbeat slowed to a throb, and his breathing became labored. He thought if he kept his distance, even when they both were at the same SAR site, he'd be all right. He'd thought they would marry after high school. When she'd eloped with Aaron, one of his good friends, he had locked away the unbearable pain of rejection. Until she'd returned to Anchorage last year. Then the lid had lifted on that pain and leaked out.

"You need to report that. Thomas is over there." Jesse waved toward his friend, then before he said something he'd regret about Lydia, he rotated away and said, "I still have one more building to inspect."

With Brutus by his side, he hastened toward the last store. As his Rottweiler sniffed around, Jesse examined the clothing store, the large plate window gone in front. Through the opening, he caught a movement out of the corner of his eye in the appliance shop next door. He pulled on Brutus's leash and headed for the place. As he peered inside, he glimpsed a door closing at the rear.

He entered the appliance store with Brutus and unsnapped his leash. "Check it."

While his K-9 moved around the large open space, Jesse removed his gun and strode toward the back exit. When he opened the door, he spied a black Chevy driving out of the parking lot. He took down the part of the license number not covered by mud. All employees, shop owners and customers were evacuated an hour ago, so why did this guy stay behind?

Going back inside, he did his own search of the premise while Brutus finished. Nothing. That was a good sign, but a troublesome feeling about the man who left nagged at him. He headed back toward Thomas who was talking with David in low tones.

Thomas wore his deadpan expression that didn't give anything away if reporters were watching. "So far we think at least twelve people were inside. I imagine more names will come in as people wonder where someone is. We have four employees and eight customers we know of at this time. We have been given the go-ahead to search the left side of the building."

Jesse and Brutus started for that area, the one where the second floor had crashed down on the first one. There was little to shore up, and it was probably where the bomb originated as well as where most of the casualties would be.

The thought of finding Lydia dead soured his stomach. He might be angry with her, but he prayed to the Lord she was alive somewhere in the rubble.

Lydia tried to drag deep breaths into her lungs, but the effort sent pain through her. Cracked or broken rib? She eased her eyes open to find debris all around her. Pinpoint streams of light filtered through the rubble.

A beam lay across her torso. Dust in the air caused her to sneeze and intensified the sharp constriction in her chest. The lack of oxygen and the pressure bearing down on her made her light-headed. Her eyelids slid close. She focused, as much as she could, on any sounds that indicated people were searching for survivors. Creaks and groans, as though the building were protesting its destruction, surrounded her, but she couldn't hear any voices.

She tried to move her legs. She couldn't do more

than wiggle her toe, which meant she wasn't paralyzed. One arm was pinned against her side, the other free. She pushed on the beam, but it wouldn't budge. The effort drained what strength she had. She stopped and concentrated on filling her lungs with at least shallow breaths.

Then thoughts began to invade her mind. Who would take care of her seventeen-year-old sister? She came back to Anchorage for Kate. When their father died in a climbing accident, Lydia finally returned for the funeral, not intending to stay except to settle her dad's affairs and move her sister back to Oklahoma where Lydia lived. None of her plans had worked out. Kate refused to leave her friends, and Lydia discovered her father left her his practice and part of the animal hospital.

Then Bree showed up to help her deal with her father's death. They had been close friends in school, and suddenly she felt as though fifteen years had vanished, and their relationship took off where it had stopped when she'd left Anchorage to elope with Aaron.

Why did You bring me back, God, only to have this happen? I was beginning to settle in again and forget why I'd left all those years ago. She'd even started to contemplate staying after Kate graduated from high school. She'd tried to hold on to her faith, but so many things happened. And now this. She didn't know what to do anymore.

Then there was Jesse, her first love. They had dated for over a year but broke up their senior year at Christmas. She'd started dating Aaron, which in retrospect was a rebound. She'd been trying to forget Jesse and made a big mistake that affected her even today. She and Aaron broke up after a few months and she and Jesse reunited—more in love than ever. But when she discovered she was pregnant with Aaron's baby, everything changed. Jesse had been devastated when she left without telling him why. Aaron's dad and her father had insisted they get married and keep the child a secret. Aaron's dad was a prominent citizen and her father was an elder in his church. She was to accompany Aaron to Stillwater where he was going to attend Oklahoma State University. As long as they did as they said, Aaron would have money to support them and his education paid for. The memories of those years married to Aaron chilled her. She'd never been so alone in her life.

What good was it to look back? It was too late to change anything. She didn't even know if the rescuers would find her.

Her head pounded like a jackhammer. With her free hand, she touched her hair and came away with bloody fingers. A darkness tugged at her. It offered comfort and peace.

Through the haze that clouded her mind, a noise penetrated her thoughts. A bark. Then another. The rescuers had found someone. Hope flared until another sound drowned out all others. A crash—something collapsing?

Brutus barked and wagged his tail. He found someone. As part of the second floor fell to the ground in the section not stabilized yet, Jesse headed for his Rottweiler. He reached the spot and caught a glimpse of something blue under the debris.

"Over here," Jesse shouted, and several rescuers without dogs climbed through the remains of the structure.

Jesse knelt by Brutus and tried to see through the rubbish. He glimpsed some more blue and began removing bricks and wood, praying the person—maybe Lydia—was alive beneath them. Jesse knew that time was against the trapped people. If they were alive and injured, their wounds could eventually lead to their death if help didn't get to them.

"I'm here," he heard faintly from below. Or was he imagining a voice that sounded like Lydia's?

"Lydia?" Jesse kept removing bricks.

"Yes. A beam is on me." The familiar voice grew a little stronger.

"This is Jesse. We're going to get you out."

"I need air, and it's getting dark."

"Okay. Let me see what I can do."

"Thanks, Jesse. I knew I could count on you." The last part of the sentence ended with a racking cough.

"Lydia, are you all right?"

"O—kay. So cold."

"You'll be out in no time." He worked as fast as he could. "Are you still all right?"

Nothing. His gut clenched.

"Get that air and camera over here," he shouted while David and Thomas hurried with his request. "Lydia is alive." He refused to acknowledge the possibility that she had died—just moments from being rescued.

He searched the debris until he found what he hoped was a hole that led to where Lydia was. He snatched the air tank and shoved the hose through the opening. *Please, God, keep her alive. We've already lost too many.* He said that over and over as he pushed the camera with a light down into another small crack. It was in moments like this that all he could do was believe the Lord was taking over.

TWO

Lydia blinked her eyes open. In the dim light, she saw the hose to the left of her. The air seemed fresher, although she still couldn't breathe too deeply without a shooting pain knifing through her.

She went in and out of consciousness to the noise of people removing the building on top of her. The sound of voices fueled her hope. Memories of that time she'd gotten lost in a cave swamped her—the fear of the dark, of being alone. She shivered. Then she remembered when she'd first seen Jesse with a flashlight, coming to her rescue. She'd rushed into his arms and wouldn't let him go until he'd pulled back, stared at her for a long moment and then kissed her for the first time.

What happened to that puppy love? She'd only been seventeen—Kate's age—but she'd never felt so close to another as in that moment.

Her eyelids were so heavy, like the beam across her torso. She closed them again, trying to think of a warm place. Every part of her was cold, as though she'd been in a refrigerator for hours, dressed in her scrubs. She hadn't even changed out of them when she'd gone to meet Bree. At least she wasn't there with her.

But the others…what of them?

Again she began to drift off.

Hold on, Lydia.

Did someone say that? Jesse?

A rush of cool air brushed over her. She looked up and saw Jesse's smiling face.

"She's alive." His grin grew. "Don't move. We'll get you out of there."

"I know," she whispered, her throat so dry she doubted Jesse could hear her.

When the rescuers finally reached her, all she could do was peer at Jesse as though she were back in the cave and he alone had come to save her. His almost-black hair was covered with a helmet. Dust and dirt coated him. He was more muscular and taller than when they'd been teenagers. When he and Thomas hoisted the beam from her, it seemed so easy for him while she couldn't budge it an inch.

Jesse's golden-brown gaze fastened on hers. Lines at the sides of his eyes deepened. "We've almost got you out, then Bree will check you before we move you. Do you want some water?" His voice held a tender note, as though he cared.

But she knew better. Since she'd returned to Anchorage they had spoken few words, only when necessary because of a search and rescue or Brutus, who she treated as the department veterinarian. "Yes" squeaked out of her mouth.

He couldn't prop her up to drink until Bree said it was okay to move her, but he did squirt some cold water into her mouth.

Nothing tasted better. She swallowed. "Again."

When Bree appeared next to her, she tried to hide the worry in her eyes, but Lydia knew Bree.

"I'm okay," Lydia murmured, her voice stronger now. "Get me out of this hole, and I'll be good as new in no time."

"I'll be the judge of that." Bree ran her hands over Lydia, especially examining the wound on her head, then put a neck brace on her. "She's okay to be lifted but be careful. Slow and easy. No jarring."

"Honey, stop telling us our job. We've done this before," David said from above, ready to take Lydia when Thomas and Jesse hoisted her up.

Jesse positioned himself at her head while Thomas was at her feet. "On the count of three."

Bree stabilized her midsection as Lydia was brought up out of the hole.

Sunlight bathed Lydia. She was put on a stretcher and carried from the rubble. The last sight she saw was Jesse's handsome face—but he wasn't smiling. Worry knitted his forehead.

Lydia gave in to the black swirling abyss beckoning her.

Lydia heard an annoying beep. Pain quickly followed, radiating from her head and chest. She moaned and lifted her eyelids halfway. A hospital room greeted her, and she remembered why she was here and hurting. She'd been in and out of consciousness since an emergency surgery to have her spleen repaired.

She wondered where her sister and Bree went. Earlier they'd been in here. Probably to grab something to eat. At least she wouldn't have to worry about Kate while she was in the hospital. She'd stay with Bree and David until Lydia was released, which she hoped was soon.

Lydia closed her eyes and tried to relax. But the second she did, visions of the bombing assailed her mind. The sound of hideous laughter right before the bomb went off. The expression on Melinda's face when she knew what was going to happen. Was she alive? The feeling of helplessness she experienced trapped under the building debris. Her heartbeat began to race. A cold clamminess blanketed her, much like when she'd been trapped.

The swish of her hospital room door opening pulled her away from the memories. Kate returning? She needed to have a few moments with her sister. When Lydia fastened her gaze on the person who entered, her pulse rate sped faster. Jesse Hunt. She wasn't prepared to see him.

He looked like he'd come straight from the crime scene. As a search and rescue worker for Northern Frontier, he'd probably work as long as he could function. The only time he'd rest was when Brutus needed to.

So why is he here?

He stopped at the end of the bed. "Bree told me you'd been awake earlier and coherent after your surgery, so I took a chance and came to talk to you."

His stiff stance and white-knuckled hands on the railing betrayed his nervousness, but his tone told her he was here in his professional capacity. Saddened by that thought, Lydia said, "Thank you for finding me."

"I was doing my job yesterday."

"Knowing the people who would be searching kept my hope alive. Have you found everyone?"

"We don't know for sure. Names of missing peo- ple are still coming in. I was hoping you could tell me how many people were in the restaurant when the bomb exploded."

"I'm not sure. Let me think." As much as she didn't want to, she tried to visualize the moments before the explosion. "Melinda, and I remember seeing another waitress. I don't know how many cooks she had in the kitchen. They're always in the back."

"How about customers?"

She had to think. She didn't want this person to get away with what he'd done. She fought the weariness that kept edging forward. "People were coming in and out. Some ordered takeout for lunch and didn't stay long. I came out of the restroom, saw Melinda seconds before the laugh track played. I'd estimate maybe nine besides me. Most of them were regulars."

"Who?"

"I don't know their names. I just see them there a lot. I go get lunch there once or twice a week…" The thought that the bistro was totally gone inundated her. She dropped her gaze to her lap, her hands quiver- ing. She balled them, but that didn't stop the trembling sweeping through her body.

"If I bring you photos, could you tell me if they were there?"

Emotions crammed her throat. She turned for her water on the bedside table, but it was too far away without leaning for it. She started to and winced from the movement.

Jesse was at her side, grabbing the plastic cup and offering it to her.

She took it, their fingers brushing, and she nearly splashed the water all over her with her shaking.

Jesse covered her hand and steadied her drink, then guided it to her mouth. The feel of his fingers against hers for more than a second jolted her. "I know this isn't something you want to talk about, but we want to recover all the bodies as quickly as possible."

"Bodies? Did anyone else survive?"

"A waitress and two cooks. We found them in the kitchen area, the waitress just inside the entrance while the cooks were across the room."

She didn't want to ask but she needed to know. "Did Melinda survive?"

"No, we ID'd her body. So far we've recovered eight bodies, including Melinda. Four people are missing, according to their families, but we haven't found them yet. The bomb squad thinks the bomb originated in the dining area where the customers were. They'll know more when the bomb fragments are all found."

"Eight dead." How did she survive when the others didn't? "I was in the hallway to the bathrooms when it went off, not in the main dining room. Do you think that protected me some?"

"Possibly. Do you know where the laughing sound came from?"

"Not sure." She closed her eyes and tried to think back to that time. Nothing. She massaged her temple, forcing herself to dig deeper beyond the pain throbbing against her skull. "I don't think from behind me. When I heard the laughter—" she shuddered "—I took two steps back. Then everything went blank."

Jesse put the cup on the bedside table. "I know this isn't easy, but anything you can remember could help us piece together what happened. We've got to stop this man."

"Nobody wants that more than me. I... I..." Tears blurred her vision. She couldn't voice what she felt, not even to herself. She remembered coming to in recovery, and all she'd wanted to do was surrender to the darkness. Stay there. But that wouldn't help. She'd learned long ago she couldn't escape from the truth.

"I'm sorry, Jesse. I'm tired. I'm sure I'll remember more later." She hoped she could. She needed to. If no one in the dining area survived the bombing except her, she might know something that could help find the culprit. But at the moment her head felt as if it would explode.

"I understand. I'll come back later."

Was that sympathy in his voice? She looked up. His expression was neutral. When she'd first returned home last year, she'd tried to talk to him about what happened all those years ago. He'd shut her down. He never acted angry or upset around her although she'd wronged him. Instead, he'd been more like a stranger. Even as a teenager, he'd kept his feelings to himself. That was part of the reason they broke up that first time at Christmas, and she began dating Aaron.

She watched him leave. But hadn't she done the same as him? When her mother left their family she'd shut off her emotions entirely. Even now she wouldn't think about the woman who had abandoned her family. She couldn't deal with that on top of everything else.

The emotions she'd kept checked while he was there gushed to the surface. Tears ran down her cheeks for the people who'd died, for her foolishness as a teenager, for the rift between her and her father and for the times she'd missed her mother so much it had hurt deeply. And now, she couldn't even remember anything to help the police.

Later that day, Jesse loaded Brutus into his crate in the back of his SUV and left the bombing scene. His dog needed a lengthy break if he was going to work late into August's twilight hours for the third straight day, searching the rubble for victims or clues to identify the type of bomb used. There were still two people unaccounted for, and he was going to pay another visit to both Lydia and the waitress who survived. Maybe one or both of them could tell him if the two missing people were at the restaurant. Thomas talked with the cooks, but they didn't know anything because they always stayed in the kitchen.

He drove toward the hospital, the bright yellow sun splashed across the sky in all God's glory. Life went on in spite of the tragedy that occurred yesterday. The death count with the bombings was climbing and so was the fear sweeping through the city. The mayor was demanding answers, and he'd gladly give him some if he had any.

The closest surveillance camera had been disabled before the bombing. The others didn't have a good angle on the entrance to the restaurant. Even if they had there were two other ways for a person to leave Melinda's Bistro—the back door where the kitchen was and the emergency exit down the hallway to the bathrooms. There were no cameras on those two places. In fact, each building targeted didn't have a lot of security. The police were urging businesses to increase their security.

When he rode the elevator up to Lydia's floor, he tried to prepare himself for seeing her again. He didn't want to think about their past, but as he neared her hospital room, he experienced relief and…joy all over again, like when he heard her through the rubble. She'd been alive. After finding several dead bodies, he'd started to think no one would be alive.

He'd thanked God he found her. He'd never felt that kind of relief. And yet, he had to keep his distance. Too much happened between them when they were teenagers. He'd grown up in a good foster home, but early on when he bounced from one family to another, he learned to keep himself apart from others. He would have to rely on that ability now.

He couldn't afford to be hurt by her again.

Pausing at the door, he lifted his hand to knock and froze. He couldn't go inside. *I've got a job to do. Get in. Get out.*

He rapped his knuckles against the wood, heard Lydia respond and pushed the door open. He'd prefer to stay at the end of the bed, but he had to show her the photos. He'd have to stand next to her, only a couple of feet away.

When he entered, a neutral expression fell over her features. Her brown eyes held a guarded look. She'd been pretty as a teenager, a little gangly, but now fifteen years later, she was a tall beauty, nothing awkward as she moved. What he'd observed at search and rescues was a self-assured woman who was aware of herself at all times. That had changed over the years. What else?

"Is this a good time to talk?" Jesse asked, almost wishing she would say no.

"Yes. Bree and Kate went to lunch. They should be back soon." Her voice, husky laden, was the same, and its sound renewed memories best forgotten. "I haven't remembered anything new. I wish I could. Everything is fuzzy. Maybe it's the meds they have me on."

"That could be. But it also may be the trauma. The waitress doesn't remember anything, either, but I wanted to show both of you the photos of the two people still missing and see if you can place them at the restaurant when the bomb went off."

"I'll try to help any way I can. I want this madman caught before others die."

"On that, we agree." But on so many other things, they hadn't agreed on. Aaron had been a good friend, but Jesse had known Aaron wouldn't be good for Lydia. Obviously she hadn't felt that way. Even after they got back together in April, out of nowhere she left Anchorage with Aaron in June.

Jesse removed the two pictures from his shirt pocket. One was of a young woman and the other an older gentleman. He laid them on the tray table. "Does either one seem familiar to you?"

"Maybe the older gentleman. There was one that came into the bistro when I was there. The woman I didn't see at all. I'd remember that red hair."

A smile tugged at his mouth. He thought back to a time Lydia had dyed her long brown hair that color and it turned out more a neon orange than red, especially toward the ends. She'd fixed it the best she could by cutting her hair short, which was the way she wore it now.

She stared at him. "I know what you're thinking. It turned out to be a good thing although I hated the stares I received those few days before I cut my hair. It's easier to keep this way." She combed her fingers through her strands.

"I tried to warn you."

"That's because you didn't like redheads."

"I liked you the way you were." But she never understood that. She'd wanted to be constantly reassured how he felt, and feelings had never been easy for him to express.

She handed him the photos. "I wasn't much help. I hope the waitress knows for sure. I'd hate for families not to know what happened to a loved one."

"Like what happened to your father?"

"Yes, not knowing one way or another when he disappeared in the wilderness was nerve-racking. Kate and I felt in limbo. I understand you were one of the K-9 teams that went out searching."

"Alex Witherspoon found your father at the bottom of the ravine." Ten days after he went missing. "That's one of the things David does. If we don't find the person right away, we don't give up. We keep going out until every possibility is covered."

"Thankfully he died instantly and didn't linger, injured and without food and water. But he shouldn't have gone in the first place. It was stupid to go by himself, especially with Kate living at home." Anger laced each word. "But then he never changed, even after Mom left us. He always did daredevil stunts, testing his limits with no regard for the family left behind."

Jesse stuck the pictures in his uniform shirt pocket. Things were getting too personal. He didn't want to go there. "Thanks for your help. I've got to show these to the waitress. If you do remember anything else, call Thomas. He's lead detective on the case."

Jesse left as quickly as he could. He'd almost told her to call him. That wouldn't have been a wise decision on his part. He was on the Laughing Bomber Task Force, but he'd leave Thomas to deal with Lydia.

The waitress was hospitalized in another corridor on the same floor. When Jesse made his way there, a code blue was issued. Several staff members hurried past him. As he neared the room, a sinking feeling took hold of him. A nurse pushing a crash cart cut him off. The door swung wide to reveal a team of medical personnel fighting to keep the waitress alive.

Jesse leaned against the wall, waiting to see if the woman made it. Only Lydia and this woman had been out in the dining room area and seen who the customers were. If she died, that only left Lydia.

THREE

"What do you mean I have to escort Lydia home from the hospital? Why don't you?" Good thing Thomas was Jesse's friend, or he'd never get away with challenging a superior's order.

Thomas started for his vehicle at the church bombing site. "Lydia requested you when I told her I wanted an officer to escort her home."

"Are we going to guard her or something?" He didn't want to be on that detail.

"Not at this time. The situation doesn't warrant the drain on our manpower although I have authorized the police to drive by and periodically check on her and the two cooks who are still alive. I don't think the cooks know much, but Lydia might. She was in the area that took the worst of the bombing. With the waitress dying, Lydia is our best chance. We're focusing all we can on finding this maniac."

"Do you think she's in danger?"

"Not at the moment. Her name hasn't been given to the press. If it gets out, we'll reconsider what to do or if the autopsy findings on the waitress who died last night indicate murder. We reviewed the surveillance tapes of people going in and out of her room and only saw staff members. The doctor has no reason at the moment to think someone killed her. She was injured more severely than Lydia." Thomas opened his car door. "I have a lead to follow up."

"Trade you?"

Thomas shook his head. "You're complaining because I asked you to make sure a beautiful woman gets home okay? I'm beginning to think you were the one who suffered a head trauma."

"Cute. You know Lydia and I have a history."

"Which is even more reason to put you with her. You know her. You know what to expect. I'm not asking you to be her new best friend."

"You owe me."

"You wanted in on this case."

"Because this was my church that was bombed." Jesse waved his arm toward where the building used to be.

"While you're with her, help her to remember. Somewhere in her mind she might have seen the bomber and can ID him. Now, that would be a lead."

Jesse watched Thomas drive away, then stormed to his police cruiser with Brutus. Before opening the rear of his SUV, he knelt next to his Rottweiler and petted him. "At least you understand why I don't want to see her. I've ranted to you enough this past year. This city of nearly three hundred thousand doesn't seem to be big enough for the both of us."

Brutus barked, then licked Jesse on his cheek.

He laughed. "I like your reply. I know I've got to do my best. Nothing less." He rubbed his hand down Brutus's back. "Load." Jesse gave the command for his K-9 to hop into the rear and crawl into his crate. He fastened the door, although in an emergency Brutus could undo the latch.

Yesterday when the other survivor had died, he'd interviewed the staff and reported it to Thomas. He'd asked the staff not to talk about the death. The police didn't want rumors flying around. With Bree at the hospital, he'd keep tabs on anything being said.

Now he'd return to take Lydia home and have the task of informing her about the waitress's death and finding the older gentleman's remains in the last area to be searched at the bomb site. Since the young woman who had been the other missing person showed up at work, everyone was accounted for.

When he arrived at Lydia's room, after dropping Brutus off at home, she sat in a wheelchair looking out the window. She glanced back at him as he entered.

"Thomas called and told me you were driving me home. I appreciate it."

He approached her and clasped the wheelchair handles to roll her out of the room. "Why did you request me?" His voice sounded even, belying his frustration.

"Because I think we should talk, and you've been doing a good job of avoiding me. We were friends once—"

"Yes, once. We aren't now."

"I realize that, but I owe you an apology. I've been meaning to talk to you since before the bomb went off. If nothing else, I can take away from this situation how fragile life is. Don't put off what you should do. In one second, a lot of people died at the hands of this madman. The more I think about what happened, the more I get the feeling I know something."

"Shh." Jesse scanned the hallway leading out of the building. "We'll talk when we arrive at your house. I don't want anyone overhearing us. We haven't released your name to the press. The bomber doesn't know who the survivors are." If that truly was the case, then the waitress died naturally.

He waited until he brought the car around and assisted Lydia into the front passenger seat to tell her about the death of the waitress. He didn't want a public reaction to the news.

On the drive to her house, after a long silence, Jesse stopped at a red light and looked at Lydia. "I didn't want to say anything until we were alone, but the waitress died last night. An autopsy is being performed to determine the cause of death."

"You don't think her death is a result of the bomb explosion?"

"Probably. She was in more critical condition than you were, but she had been responding to treatment and improving so I can't say for sure."

"What does the press know?"

"How many died in the blast and that there were four survivors. No names at this time because we were still identifying victims and notifying family. That will change now since everyone is accounted for."

Lydia stared out the windshield. "You think I might be in danger?"

"I hope not, but it's a possibility if the bomber thinks you can ID him. That's why we won't release your name, but the press have their ways of finding out."

"I can't. Yet. But what if I did see him and I can't remember?"

"You suffered a head trauma. Not remembering,

especially right away, isn't uncommon. Don't force yourself. If you have any information, it'll come to you in time."

"Are you sure you work for the police? I'd think you should be pushing me to remember right now."

When the light turned green, he threw her a half grin and pressed on the accelerator. "I know you. Force won't work."

"I've been trying, and I can remember a few bits like how Melinda looked when she heard the laugh track, how I felt when I did. After that nothing and not much else before other than remembering Bree thankfully left ten minutes before the bomb went off."

"Yes, I talked with Bree. She remembered some of the people we found in the rubble."

"Lunch was starting. The door opened and closed—four times after she was gone." She shifted toward him. "I just thought of that."

He glanced at her smile, which lit her whole face. He'd always loved seeing her grin from deep inside her. "See. It will come."

"I feel like I need to remember right now because someone else might die if he strikes again."

"We're interviewing a lot of people who were there earlier or on that street sometime that morning. You're not our only hope."

Jesse pulled into her driveway, the same house he would pick her up at as a teenager. A memory flashed into his mind—of kissing her on the front porch. Eons ago when he was a different person. His chest tightened. He wouldn't go down that path again.

"I'll see you to your door."

"Will you stay until Kate comes home from school?"

"I—I…" He didn't want to be with her any more than necessary, but one look into her pale face and he couldn't say no. "Fine. When does she get home? I'll need to let Thomas know what I'm doing."

Lydia checked the clock on the dashboard. "No more than an hour. She carpools with a few friends."

As they walked slowly toward the house, Jesse just thought of something. "How are you going to get in? Your purse was destroyed by the bomb."

She slipped her hand into her jean pocket and pulled out a key. "Bree had the locks changed and gave a key to me and Kate. Alex went grocery shopping for me, so I won't have to do that right away. My friends have been so helpful, especially with Kate. Reconnecting with Bree and Alex when I came back to Anchorage has made my return home easier." Lydia opened her front door and entered.

Jesse followed, scanning the house. He was glad he'd taken Brutus home so he could run and play in his large fenced backyard. These past days, his K-9 had worked long hours and needed the break.

Lydia dropped the small bag of clothes Bree had brought her in the hospital on a chair in the spacious living room and walked through the dining room toward the kitchen. "I'm fixing myself a good cup of tea. What they had at the hospital isn't what I call tea. Do you want some?"

"I'm a coffee drinker. No, thanks."

As he strolled through the house, snatches of his time spent here continued to bombard him. Lydia always had to come right home from school to babysit her little sister who stayed with a neighbor until Lydia arrived. Her dad didn't get off work until six and sometimes didn't come home right away. Lydia hated being alone and usually their friends would gather at her place.

Jesse caught sight of a recent photo of Lydia with her younger sister. Picking up the framed picture, he realized he hadn't seen much of Kate since those early years. She looked a lot like Lydia at the same age. Quickly he returned the photograph to the end table.

Why had he agreed to stay until Kate got home? He didn't want to be pulled into Lydia's world again, and yet he had allowed himself to be persuaded to wait an hour.

"I have some…" Lydia opened the refrigerator "…I guess only water. Kate likes soft drinks, but there are none in here."

"Water is fine." He remained in the entrance of the dining room until the memory of sharing Thanksgiving dinner with Lydia and her family a few weeks before they broke up their senior year faded. He stood at the bay window that overlooked the unfenced backyard with woods a hundred yards from the house.

"Do you still get moose around here?"

"Yes, also caribou and occasionally a bear. That's why I keep the garbage cans in the garage except on pickup day."

"Have you had any trouble with them?" He could do a generic conversation with Lydia. Nothing too personal.

"Kate's an animal lover and takes photos of all our visitors. Once she was at the window in her bedroom, snapping a picture when the bear came over and tried to get inside. He tore the screen, and we had to replace it. The way she screamed, I thought the bear was inside. I ran and got my dad's gun, then went to rescue her." She appeared behind him.

Jesse pivoted from the window, and the familiar scent of apple floated to him. She held out the glass of water, and he took it.

But she remained where she was—too close. When she looked up at him, for a few seconds the years apart fell away, and he was a teenager again and in love for the first time.

Then she smiled, and no one else existed for that moment. It was as if fifteen years vanished along with all the hurts and words exchanged between them.

The shrill whistle of the kettle pierced the air. Lydia gasped as though she'd been transfixed as much as he had.

When she crossed to the stove to make her tea, he sat in a chair and took deep sips of his iced water, relishing the cold liquid. "What happened with the bear?"

"I closed the blackout curtains and hoped he would forget that we were inside. He hit the screen a couple more times, then left. We both collapsed on the bed, laughing."

"Laughing?"

"In relief that we were still alive. I'd been checking out the bedroom door and wondering if that would stop a bear if he did get into the house through the window. I'd decided no."

Chuckling, Jesse relaxed, surprised by both actions.

When Lydia returned to the kitchen table and sat across from him, she blew on her tea and took a sip, a habit she'd had since he'd first known her. What else did she still do? She used to chew on her thumbnail when she was nervous. He looked at her hand and saw each fingernail was cut short.

"I'm glad you're having a good laugh over my bear encounter. There is a downside to living a little ways out from the main part of the city. More wildlife."

"To me that's what's appealing about this place. I live in town with a fenced yard. Brutus needs to have a place to exercise when he isn't working. I can't risk him encountering a bear."

Lydia shifted in her chair and cringed. "I'm trying to ignore my bruised ribs, but they love reminding me they've been mistreated."

"Being in that hallway protected you some from the main blast."

She stared at her tea, tracing her finger around the rim. "I know. I…" She shook her head. "Can we not talk about the bombing?"

"You need to remember, and talking sometimes helps."

Her mouth tightened. "Not right now. When I start trying to think about that day, my mind shuts down."

"That's not an unusual reaction for a traumatic experience. So what do you want to talk about, if not the case?"

"The way things ended for us. I never wanted to hurt you. If I could have done that over—"

He held up his hand. "Don't. We can't change what happened and discussing it to death won't help. What was done is done."

"I understand, but ignoring something doesn't make it disappear."

"Maybe I want to be reminded to be cautious."

"With me?" Her eyes darkened. "I made a couple of

big mistakes as a teenager and have learned a lot from them. I hope we can be friends at least."

Friends. That was how things started originally. "Listen, I'm sorry it didn't work out with you and Aaron, but when you eloped it changed everything."

A noise from the foyer charged the air between them.

"Lydia, I'm home. Where are you?"

"I'm in the kitchen."

He stood, the sound of his chair scraping across the floor echoing through the kitchen. "I need to check in with Thomas before I call it a day. I'd better leave. I'll lock the door on my way out." He passed Kate in the dining room, nodding at her but not slowing his step.

Always in the back of his mind, he wondered why she'd married Aaron so fast after going out with him again. He'd thought they really had a chance to make it work that second time. He was a foster kid while Aaron came from a good family with some influence in Anchorage. Had money in the end meant something to Lydia? Or was it something else that changed her mind? They had started to make up after their breakup at Christmas, but in a snap of his finger, everything had fallen apart. And Jesse had only himself to rely on, again.

Lydia forced a smile when Kate came into the kitchen. The sound of the front door slamming came just as Lydia realized she'd have to tell Jesse the whole sordid incident of her becoming pregnant and having to marry Aaron. One foolish night and her whole life had changed. She lost so much then. Although she'd communicated with Kate on a regular basis over the years, they weren't close. And her father had made it clear she wasn't welcome in Anchorage.

"How was school?"

Kate shrugged. "Nothing earth-shattering. Everyone is still talking about the bombing. They're scared."

"So am I."

"They've locked down the school tight. No one gets inside without a valid reason and everyone gets searched at the main entrance."

"Good. I'm glad they're taking precautions. I imagine other places will, too."

Kate went to the refrigerator and looked inside. "We shouldn't have to live in fear like this. Have you remembered anything?"

She already felt pressured. She hated that it was also coming from Kate. "I'm trying." Lydia took her cup to the sink. "I'm going to lie down. Just doing this little has worn me out."

"Can we order pizza tonight?"

"Sure. That way I don't have to come up with something." Lydia left the kitchen while Kate sliced cheese to put on crackers.

Emotionally and physically drained, Lydia moved slowly toward her bedroom at the end of the hallway. Luckily there were no steps to climb.

Crossing to the dresser, she decided to get comfortable and put on her pajamas, although it was only four thirty in the afternoon. In fact, she might sleep most of the evening and only get up to eat pizza, which she loved.

After she took a pair of pj's out, she swung around, her gaze skimming over the items on her desk as she made her way to the bathroom connected to her bedroom. She stopped and stared at the wooden surface. Something was wrong. Her cup of pens seemed askew. Her desk didn't look ransacked, but it didn't look right. A shiver wracked her weakened body. Someone had gone through her desk.

FOUR

Lydia racked her brain trying to figure out what felt so wrong. She hugged herself and rubbed her hands up and down her arms. Didn't she close the top drawer all the way? She always did. Keeping everything neat and in order helped her get through her busy schedule.

"What's wrong?" Kate lounged against the door-jamb, popping the last bite of her cheese and cracker into her mouth.

Lydia pointed a shaky forefinger at the drawer slightly ajar. "Did you get something from my desk?"

Kate frowned and straightened, squaring her shoulders. "I didn't go through your desk. Bree and I came in here and got some clothing for you, but that was all. Why do you think I would?" Anger edged Kate's words.

Lydia stepped closer and pulled the drawer open. She spied the notebook with a snow scene on the cover inside and sighed. It was still there. Every night she would write in it and then put it up, shutting the drawer. Not that there were any big secrets in her journal, but the idea someone else read her innermost thoughts made her blood go cold. It was one place where she would let everything out.

Lydia shut the drawer completely and looked toward Kate. "Sorry. I must have left it open. I'm such a creature of habit I thought someone had been in here going through the desk. Do you remember when you were getting the clothes if it was ajar?"

"I don't even remember looking at the desk. I know you have a place for everything, but maybe you were upset and for once didn't close it all the way."

The last time she wrote in her journal, Lydia had poured her heart out about the fight she and her little sister had over a boy Kate was dating. Lydia shook her head. She'd said some things that she regretted. To say there was tension between them after their argument concerning Connor was an understatement.

Kate surveyed the room. "Is anything missing?"

Lydia didn't get thrown off her game easily, but when she did she had trouble regaining focus. Her attention fixed on her laptop, sitting exactly as she would have left it sitting on the top of her desk. "Not that I can see. I guess with all that has happened lately, I'm jumpy. But still…" She stared at the drawer, not able to shake the thought she was right. No, it was only her overactive mind. Obviously she'd gone through a traumatic experience she hadn't dealt with yet and was imaging problems when there weren't any.

"Maybe you should call Sergeant Hunt. Let him know. He's been working on your case."

"And say what?" Lydia walked around the room, opening and closing other drawers. "Nothing seems to be gone. My most valuable possession in here is my laptop, and it's on the desk." When she looked into her walk-in closet, she stiffened. Clothes and hangers were tossed on the floor.

"Maybe I should call him. My closet is a mess," Lydia murmured before she could stop herself.

Kate came up behind her and glanced over Lydia's shoulder. She flinched at her little sister's quiet approach and stepped back.

Kate pushed past her into the closet and began picking up the shirts and pants.

"Leave it. It could be evidence."

Clenching a blouse in her hand still on its hanger, Kate glared at her. "I did this. I was upset and hurrying to get back to the hospital. I was looking for the green shirt you like to wear because it's so comfortable. I thought you could wear it home."

Her tension deflated, Lydia sagged against the door, holding herself upright. "I'll take care of it later. Right now I just want to lie down." She made her way to her bed and sank back against the pillows. "I'm sorry I accused you of going through my desk."

"Yeah, right." Kate huffed and stomped into the hallway.

I should get up and go after her. But exhaustion swamped Lydia. She closed her eyes and decided she would in a little while after Kate calmed down. After Lydia rested…

As Jesse drove toward the bistro bomb site after being at Lydia's, he couldn't shake from his mind the brief conversation about that last year before she eloped with Aaron and didn't return to Anchorage. All he wanted to do was forget it. Why did women always want to discuss things to death? The past was just that.

And as far as he and Lydia being friends, he didn't see that as an option. He didn't want her to hurt him again. It was like when he was a young boy and touched the hot stove. He never did it again. Once was enough to teach him to stay away.

Thomas wanted Jesse to follow up with the appliance store's owner today. The black Chevy with the partial license plate number Jesse had written down hadn't been found yet.

Not long after the bombing, Thomas had sent two police officers to interview each store owner on the street. Yesterday Officer Williams hadn't been able to get much from Mr. Pickens, the man who owned the appliance store. He'd been so shaken up that he could barely remember anything about that morning. This was the first day the police had allowed people back on the street after another thorough search for a follow-up bomb or any evidence. Besides Mr. Pickens, Jesse would also interview the manager at the clothing store and drugstore next door.

Jesse parked in front of Pickens Appliance, and after retrieving Brutus from the back, entered the shop. He immediately homed in on the tall, overweight man watching two men measure the area where the plate glass window used to be.

Jesse approached Mr. Pickens, recognizing him from his driver's license photo. "Mr. Pickens, I'm Sergeant Hunt, and I need to have a few words with you about the day of the bombing."

"I was in the back when the bomb went off. Shook the whole building. By the time I came out of the office, everyone was fleeing, screaming, scared."

"When did you leave that day?" Jesse gave Brutus a short leash and signaled for him to sit next to him.

"When you guys asked us to evacuate the area. I wasn't gonna wait for another bomb to go off."

"I checked your store not long after noon and found someone in here. He fled out the back. Do you have any idea who it could have been? An employee? A customer who didn't leave?"

"Everyone was gone when I locked up. Don't know why I bothered because all any person had to do was climb through the window." Mr. Pickens waved his hand toward the large gap at the front of the building. "We spent all morning picking up the glass. It shattered everywhere."

"Do you have a surveillance camera in here?"

The man pointed to two mounted cameras. "They don't work. It's not like someone is going to shoplift a stove. What did the person look like that you saw?"

"I got a brief glimpse of a dark hoodie before the door shut. When I looked out back, all I saw was a black Chevy driving away. Couldn't tell you the year. Do you remember seeing anyone park there that morning?"

"No, but it was here when I came to work at ten. I thought it belonged to an employee of the stores next to me. Like I said, I was in my office most of the time on the phone to the bank."

"Who were the employees working the floor that day?"

"Bill Campbell and myself."

"So Bill is here?"

Mr. Pickens nodded. "He's the one with the broom."

Jesse approached Bill Campbell, a medium-sized lanky guy, with a sour expression on his face. After introducing himself, Jesse asked, "I understand you were on the floor the morning the bomb went off across the street. Did you see anything strange? Someone hanging around watching the building?"

He stopped sweeping and leaned on the broom. "It wasn't busy that morning. We usually get more customers in the afternoon or evening. There was a woman in here looking, but she wasn't here when the bomb went off. Don't know her name. Then there was a young man, maybe twenty-five in here. He wandered around looking at all kinds of appliances." Campbell stared at the hole where the window used to be. "You know he kept looking out front as if he was waiting for someone."

"Do you know his name?"

"Nope but he was here when the bomb went off."

"Did he leave right away?"

"I don't know. I was hiding behind the counter. When I finally stood up, all I focused on was the bistro."

"Would you be able to describe the man to a police artist?"

Campbell's eyes grew round. "You think he had something to do with the bombing?"

"I'm looking into everything."

"I'll do what I can. We've got to catch this guy before another bomb goes off. Business was slow before this last bomb. I don't expect much now."

"Will you be here tomorrow?"

"Yes."

"I'll send the police artist then." Jesse shook Campbell's hand, then left with Brutus.

Jesse visited the clothing shop then the drugstore, flanking Pickens Appliance. Neither place had any

promising leads. The few employees in those establishments were scared and jumpy. Phillip Keats, the
pharmacist and manager, even told him one longtime
woman employee called in sick and hadn't returned
since the bombing.

As he strolled to his SUV his phone rang. It was
Lydia's house number. He quickly answered, praying
nothing was wrong. "Lydia?"

"No, this is Kate."

"Has something happened?"

"Lydia thought someone had been in her bedroom.
I'm scared."

Jesse turned on his engine. "Is anyone there now?"

"No, but—"

"I'll be there as soon as possible." After discon-
necting, Jesse pulled out of his parking space. Why
didn't Lydia call him? *Because you told her to contact
Thomas.* He realized the foolhardiness of that. They
might not be friends now, but they were close once. He
couldn't walk away because she hurt him in the past—
not if her life was in jeopardy.

*A sea of black surrounded her, but Lydia couldn't
move. Something held her down. Her heartbeat began
to race. She couldn't breathe.*

Lydia's eyes flew open. Darkness blanketed her.
A band felt as though it constricted her chest. Panic
drove her off the bed. But when she stood, she began
to see shapes and glimpsed the clock. It was 9:30—
obviously at night. She wasn't trapped any longer. She
was safe and at home.

Just a dream—no, a nightmare.

She flipped on the overhead light and drank in

the sight of her bedroom. She eased onto the bed and dragged deep breaths into her lungs until her heartbeat slowed to a normal rate.

Quiet melted the tension that had gripped her, and she thought of going back to sleep. But immediately dismissed that notion. She'd already slept over four hours, and her stomach rumbled. She decided to check on Kate and see if she'd ordered that pizza.

Thoughts of her sister brought back what happened earlier and the fact that Kate was no doubt angry with her, her usual attitude toward Lydia. She hadn't handled her sister right. She needed to apologize. She didn't want what happened to disrupt her life any more than it already had.

Out in the hallway, she found Cheri waiting at her door. Scooping her cat up into her arms, she started for the living room. The sound of Kate's voice as well as a deep, masculine one floated to her. Who was here? She hoped it wasn't the boy Kate was dating. Connor was a senior and from what she'd discovered, wild. Lydia didn't want her sister making the mistake she'd made.

She followed the voices to the kitchen. Stopping in the entrance, she stared first at Brutus, then Jesse sitting at the table with Kate across from him.

"Are you sure you don't want any more pizza? Lydia might not wake up until morning." Kate was finishing off a piece, then slurped a long sip of her soft drink.

Jesse's gaze snagged Lydia's.

Kate twisted around in her chair and looked at Lydia. "How long have you been there?"

She moved into the kitchen, Cheri wiggling in her arms. "A few seconds. Why?" She placed her cat on the floor, and Cheri stared at Brutus, then walked to him and settled down beside the Rottweiler as though that was where she belonged. Brutus gave her cat one look and closed his eyes.

Kate shrugged. "Just wondering."

What had they been talking about? Lydia switched her attention to Jesse, his expression his usual neutral one whenever they were around each other. "Why are you here? Has something happened on the case?"

Jesse and Kate exchanged a glance. "Kate called me."

"How? Why?" Her sister had met Jesse at the hospital and had seen him again when she'd come home from school earlier, but that had all been casual.

Kate scraped the chair back and shot to her feet, rounding on Lydia. "I called Bree and she gave me Jesse's number. I started thinking about how someone might have been in the house, and I got scared."

"Why didn't you wake me up?"

"And you'd do what? You're hurting. Bree was working, and David is tied up. I thought of asking Connor to come over, but then you'd freak out if you found him here."

If she'd seen Connor, she probably would have. Connor reminded her of Aaron, and she didn't want her sister to have anything to do with him, especially when she was sound asleep in another room. "I was wrong. I'm sure no one has been in the house while we were gone. The evening before the bombing, I was late going to bed, and I just didn't shut the drawer all the way. I can't even remember what happened at the bistro, let alone the night before." *I'm panicking at the small things*.

Kate curled her hands and then uncurled them.

"Yeah, I guess. Anyway, I've got homework." She looked over her shoulder at Jesse. "Thanks for sitting here with me."

"No problem." He gave her a smile that died the second Kate left the kitchen.

Leaving them alone.

The past few minutes left Lydia drained. She sank onto the chair Kate had vacated. Brutus came over and put his head in her lap. She began stroking him, and the feel of his fur soothed her. Finally she looked up at Jesse, studying him.

"You should have called Thomas if you thought there was a chance someone was in your house."

"But not you," came out, and she wished she could take those words back. Even she could hear the regret in them. Cheri jumped up on the table and purred, then plopped down in front of Lydia while Brutus lay on the floor by her chair.

Jesse glanced out the window over the sink.

When she could no longer take the silence, Lydia made a decision. Right now she felt her life had shattered into hundreds of fragments. "I can't change what happened, but I'm asking you to put what happened right after graduation in the past. I could use a friend right now."

He swung his attention to her, but she couldn't read anything in his expression. "What about Bree or Alex?"

"You knew me better than anyone did at one time."

One eyebrow rose. "Did I? I used to think I did, but then you took off. One day you were here. The next gone and married."

"I called you and left a message on your voice mail."

"Yeah, at the airport right before you got on the plane to leave. With no real explanation."

Stress knotted her shoulders and neck, the pain surpassing the ache from her bruised ribs. She remembered the tears she'd cried when she'd agreed to marry Aaron and leave. The disappointment on her father's face was engraved in her mind—a vision she couldn't shake even after all these years. She'd let everyone down, but mostly Jesse. He deserved better than her.

She swallowed several times, but still her throat was as dry as the ground in the midst of a severe drought. She walked to the sink and drank some water, then returned to the table, combing her fingers through Cheri's thick white fur. "I couldn't because we'd promised our parents we wouldn't tell anyone."

"What? That you were eloping?"

"That I was pregnant with—Aaron's child."

For a few seconds his mouth pressed together in a thin, hard line, and his eyes darkened. Then as though he realized he was showing his anger a shutter descended over his features. But she saw a tic in his jawline.

Finally after a long moment, he asked, "Where's your child? With Aaron?"

That he would even think she'd let Aaron have full custody of her child devastated her. She rose, gripping the edge of the table and leaning into it. "I lost my little girl when I was seven months pregnant. I had to deliver her stillborn." She spun on her heel and stalked toward the hallway.

She heard the sound of the chair being scooted across the tiles, and all she could think about was getting away from him before she fell apart and poured out the pain she'd locked deep inside.

He caught up with her and clasped her arm, stopping her escape. "I'm sorry, Lydia. I know how much you wanted children."

A houseful, she'd once told him when they'd talked about the future. "Dreams have a way of changing," she whispered, remembering the few times she'd dated after her divorce from Aaron. No one had been Jesse. Instead, she'd thrown her life into her career and her love of animals.

"Yes, I know." His hand fell away from her.

And she missed his touch. For a second, she'd felt connected to him again like when they were teenagers.

"Why didn't you come back to Alaska?"

"I was married to Aaron and I took that seriously. I wanted to make our marriage work even after our daughter died."

"What happened?"

"He had an affair with one of his professors while I worked to support us and allowed him to go to college full-time."

"He came back here a couple of years ago with an older woman as a traveling companion. He talked with Thomas but didn't get in touch with me." One corner of his mouth hitched up. "Good thing, too, even though I didn't know all the details of your elopement." He swept his arm toward the table. "I'll warm up some pizza while we talk about what happened earlier. Kate had herself worked up by the time I arrived."

His softer expression coupled with his coaxing voice urged her to accept, especially because she was hungry. "That sounds nice. Food was what drew me out here in the first place."

After Jesse heated up the remaining slices and fixed a cup of tea for Lydia, he sat across from her. As she took several bites, he finally asked, "Explain again why you initially felt someone had been in your house. I've taken a look around and haven't seen a forced point of entry. I was surprised you didn't have a dog or two until your assistant brought the cats."

She placed Cheri on the floor, then took several sips of her warm tea. "I had Bree take both of my cats to the veterinary hospital for boarding. I didn't want her to have to deal with them and Kate. JoAnn, my assistant who brought them home, told me they were being thoroughly spoiled. Charlie and Cheri are siblings left at the back door of the hospital. One look into Cheri's green eyes and I knew I had to keep them."

"No guard dog?"

She shook her head. "But Charlie growls like a dog, and anytime someone comes to the house, he's at the door growling."

"That's better than nothing."

"Yeah, but as soon as the person comes in, he runs and hides, whereas Cheri is all over the visitor. She's never met a stranger."

"So that's why I've only seen her." Flipping his hand at Cheri, Jesse relaxed. "I'm surprised you have cats. You always had a dog growing up."

"The cats needed me." *And I needed them.* It had been within a month of her arrival in Anchorage. She'd been dealing with a hostile sister, who was grieving but not expressing those emotions. Many nights she'd been up late cuddling Cheri and talking to her about her day. In those first months she and Kate had argued every day. At least now it wasn't as often.

"Tell me about going into your bedroom."

"I didn't notice anything at first, but when I looked at my desk, I saw the top drawer was open about an inch or two. I always make sure I close drawers and cabinets. Remember when I fractured my wrist?"

"Oh, yeah. You told me you fell, not how."

"I'd opened the drawer a few minutes before, then the phone rang and I was in a hurry to answer it, but I rammed right into the drawer and fell. It's become second nature to me to shut them now, which is why it stood out, but I couldn't find anything missing or out of order. I was upset, so I supposed I could have forgotten to shut the drawer. The night before Kate and I had a big fight over Connor. That boy isn't good for her, but she won't listen to me."

"And you find that strange?" A grin twitched the corners of his mouth.

"Okay, you don't have to remind me about my dad and me. He changed so much after Mom left, and I could be stubborn."

"You think?"

She narrowed her eyes and pinched her lips together but couldn't maintain the tough act. She started chuckling. "I seem to remember you could be quite determined, too."

"Still am, and I'm especially determined to catch this person setting off the bombs. If you don't mind, I didn't check out your room earlier. May I look at it?"

"Sure." She frantically reviewed how it looked and breathed a little easier when she remembered everything was neat and put away—except for the clothes on the closet floor.

"Do you want me to check it out now?"

"I have something I need to do first, then you can."

"I don't care if it's messy."

"I do."

"A mess you made?"

"No, Kate did when she was getting something for me to wear home from the hospital. The clothes I came to the ER in were given to the police and then I hope thrown away."

"Nothing is going to be tossed until this case is over. The police are scouring each bomb site for any clue to who is behind this. Because this bomber is so erratic we can't predict where he will go next."

For a few seconds the sound of the laugh track blared through her mind. She shook. "So you think he will strike again?"

"Yes."

The one word froze her as though a blizzard swept through her kitchen. And somewhere in her memory she might have a picture of the killer. If only she could remember...

"Are you okay?"

Jesse's question pulled her from her thoughts. "I want to remember what happened at the bistro, but the more I try, the harder it is."

"Then don't try. It will come to you."

"But in time to stop another bombing?"

He reached across the table and took her hand. "We're working on the case. A lot of manpower and resources are going into this. You might not have seen anything. Don't do that to yourself."

He was right. She had enough guilt to handle without adding to it. She and her dad never really reconciled their differences before he died. That was why her relationship with Kate was so important. She didn't want to have that regret again. She could even apply that to Jesse. She didn't see their relationship returning to the way it was, but she wanted to mend it enough to remain friends.

"I'm trying, but then I think of the people I was acquainted with who died in the bombing and it's hard not to put pressure on myself."

"You suffered a severe concussion. It takes time for your brain to heal."

She inhaled a deep breath and was reminded it would take time for her ribs to heal, too. "Give me a couple of minutes to pick up the clothes. My bedroom is the last one on the right."

A minute later, she bent over in her closet to scoop up the clothes, but as she straightened, she winced. She was constantly rethinking how to move to keep from sending pain through her chest. Not an easy task when she was used to being on the go. After hanging the shirts and pants up, she surveyed the floor for any signs that meant someone besides her sister could have been in here. Everything appeared as she'd left it. At least from what she could remember.

She emerged from the closet to find Jesse in the entrance while Cheri sauntered into the room and jumped up on her bed. His gaze captured hers, and for a moment she couldn't think of anything to say. Transfixed by his presence, the seconds ticked off until he finally dragged his attention away and took in the room. He crossed to each of the windows and checked to make sure they were locked. She should have thought of that. When he walked to the desk and opened the top drawer, she tensed, but he didn't touch or say anything.

"Nothing seems unusual. The windows are locked, and I can't find any evidence of tampering. Who has a key to your house besides Bree?"

"No one except Kate and Bree."

"Nothing outside under a rock or something?" Lines at the corners of his eyes deepened, drawing her full attention to their color, a heart-melting caramel, her favorite candy.

"No. Kate lost her key once, and she had to call me at the animal hospital to come home and open the door."

"When?"

"Months ago, but I changed the locks since she never found it." She started for the hallway, needing to put some space between her and Jesse. There had been a reason she'd kept her distance between them this past year. Seeing him made her regret even more what she did, and now they were different people. After Aaron, she didn't trust easily. While she'd dedicated herself to their relationship, he'd been having an affair that destroyed their three-year marriage.

Kate opened her door across the hall from Lydia's room. Her sister glanced from her to Jesse. "I can get you some bedding for the couch in the living room. It's very comfortable."

Lydia stood in front of Jesse, who was still in her doorway. "What do you mean, Kate?"

"Jesse said he would stay if he thought someone had been in our house."

"But we've decided I overreacted and no one was.

He doesn't have to stay." Although the idea had merit, and she would have asked if she really thought someone had been in the house, it was still clear he was uncomfortable around her. She'd offered a partial explanation of what happened years ago, but they really hadn't discussed it.

"You might feel all right, but I don't. What if you had died?" Tears filled Kate's eyes, and she whirled around and disappeared into her bedroom, slamming the door.

FIVE

Lydia stared at the closed door, understanding the emotions her sister was going through. She was still experiencing a gauntlet of feelings, ranging from anger to dismay to sadness, each striking her over and over.

Jesse cleared his throat. "Lydia, go talk to her. I'll wait in the living room with Brutus."

"Thanks. She was pretty quiet at the hospital. At least now she's talking about how she's feeling." She approached the bedroom, hoping she could find the right words to say to her sister. She didn't want this to make a bigger mess out of their relationship.

After rapping on the door, she fortified herself with thoughts that could bring them closer together. Something good could come out of this tragedy.

"Go away," Kate shouted.

Lydia knocked again.

Suddenly the door was wrenched open, and Kate's usual glare pierced through Lydia. Right now her sister's anger was front and center. It was hard to reason with her when she was like this. Had Lydia been this difficult for her dad? Was this why they had always butted heads? "I'd like to come in and talk."

"Why? You never listen to me. You aren't my parent."

"No, I'm your guardian, but that has nothing to do with what we need to talk about."

Kate stepped to the side and let her enter the room. At least she didn't slam the door this time. Lydia sat on her bed, exhaustion creeping in.

"Why did you really call Jesse? Other than my initial reaction, there wasn't any indication someone had been in our house."

She fisted her hands. "Only a few survived the bombing. What if the bomber comes after you? What if..." Kate's voice thickened, and she swung around and stared at the laptop and papers on her desk.

"I don't remember anything. I'm not a threat to him."

"But you could be." Kate's back was still to Lydia.

She pushed off the bed and closed the space between them. She started to touch her sister's shoulder, but her stiff stance told her to keep away. "If it'll make you feel better, I'll have Jesse stay the night, but we need to move on and put this behind us because that solution is only temporary." She almost laughed at that statement. She didn't know if she'd be able to do that, but she didn't want Kate to be afraid. "He has a job to do. He's on the task force looking for the bomber. I want him to be a hundred percent rested."

Kate slowly turned. "So do I, but he has to sleep somewhere. Why not here?"

Because I can't deal with that. I wronged him and every time I see him that's reinforced. "Let's take it one day at a time," was all Lydia could come up with, which really wasn't a solution. But she didn't have the energy to hash this out with Kate tonight. "I'll ask him to stay…" an idea popped into her head "…or better yet, I'll have him leave Brutus here if he's willing to. I've treated Brutus, and he knows me. The dog could sleep in your room."

"I'm not the one the bomber would be after. You are."

"How about Brutus sleeps in the hallway between our rooms?"

Her sister's frown melted. "Okay."

Lydia left Kate to talk with Jesse. She wasn't sure he would agree, but all she could do was ask. When she entered the living room, Jesse knelt next to his Rottweiler and was rubbing his stomach and play wrestling.

"You've got a good dog. Well trained."

Jesse peered toward her and smiled. "Yeah. We work well together."

"Kate is still scared even though I told her we didn't think anything happened here. I believe it's all leftover emotions from the day of the bombing. With our dad dying last year, she had her legs knocked out from under her. My death would have been a second big blow in a short time."

At the mention of her possible death, Jesse's eyes widened slightly and his grin dissolved. "I can certainly understand that. I was a foster kid. You not only have to deal with your parents' death but living with strangers."

As a teenager, Jesse rarely mentioned living with a foster family. In fact, he wouldn't talk about his past, something that had frustrated her because she wanted to know everything about him. "Would it be possible to leave Brutus overnight with us? It might put Kate's mind at peace."

"What about tomorrow night and the one after that?"

She pushed her fingers through her hair. "I'm hoping when nothing happens she'll begin to calm down. Right now I'm taking it one day at a time." Because that was about all she could handle. "That way you can go home and get a good night's sleep. The couch is okay but not as good as a bed. I know you've been working long hours…" Her voice faded as Jesse rose and cut the distance between them.

"I'll do what is needed. If you want me to stay, I'll make do with the couch. I love to go camping, and the hard ground is way worse."

His very nearness robbed her of any reply. She moistened her lips and stepped back. "She was happy when I suggested Brutus sleep here. It'll be easier to transition back to being just the two of us." And easier on her. She hadn't spent this much time with Jesse since they were dating.

"Then we'll do that. He doesn't eat until the morning. I'll bring his food over before I go to work. If there's a problem, call." He slipped his card into her hand, his fingers lingering a couple of seconds longer than necessary.

His touch set off a myriad of buried emotions flowing through her. "I'll take good care of Brutus."

"I know. I've seen you with the SAR dogs." His gaze snagged hers and bound her to him as though with invisible ropes.

Her heartbeat accelerated. She turned away and headed for the front door.

Jesse called Brutus and put on his leash. "I'll take him for a walk since you don't have a fenced-in backyard. It won't take long."

While Jesse and his K-9 descended the porch steps, Lydia made her way outside to stand and wait for them to return. In the darkness, she could study Jesse without him seeing. She always loved the fluid way he moved, usually as though he didn't have a care in the world. But then she'd seen him in action, quick to do whatever was needed.

When he ascended the steps with Brutus five minutes later, Lydia walked toward him and schooled her features into a neutral expression—at least she hoped, because light streamed from the open door.

"I'll need to come by early. We'll finish up at the bistro hopefully tomorrow and what remains will be for the crime scene techs to handle."

"Everyone was accounted for?"

"Yes, finally. But Brutus is a bomb detector, and we're making sure we have all the pieces left. Any evidence we can gather will help us find this guy."

"I'll be up early. I'll take Kate to school, then I'm going to the animal hospital."

"I thought the doctor told you to take it easy."

She chuckled. "You know me. When have I ever done that? I'm not staying long, but I want to check on the dog I operated on the day of the bombing. I know a lot of the staff want to see me, too. I promised Bree I would wait to go back full-time until next week."

"Okay. I'll be here by seven thirty. I'll wait to leave until you and Brutus are inside."

She strolled toward the door and glanced back. "Thank you." Maybe they could be friends again. She hoped so.

Then Jesse said, "I became a police officer to protect others. Stay, Brutus."

In other words, he was only doing his job. Jesse had a way of reminding her their time together as a couple was over. She knew that in her mind, but her heart was struggling with it.

In the living room, she watched him drive away, then switched off the lights and went into the kitchen to make sure there was water in a bowl for Brutus. In the garage she had an old cushion that she would use as a bed for Brutus. After he was settled in the hallway, she finally sank onto her bed. Jesse's parting words ran over and over through her mind. She couldn't blame him. She deserved them. She was a victim in one of his cases, and that was all.

After Jesse picked up Brutus, Lydia dropped off Kate at school, and then she drove to the animal hospital and parked in the lot on the side of the building. As she walked toward the front entrance, she stared at the bomb site where the bistro had been. She noticed Jesse's SUV near it. When he came to get Brutus, she'd invited him to have breakfast, but he'd declined. She wished he hadn't because she and Kate had argued about having the Rottweiler back that night.

Lydia hadn't slept much the night before, not because she was scared but because of Jesse. She hoped she could forget about him long enough to take a long nap.

As she entered the reception area, she came to a stop. Streamers and balloons hung from the ceiling with a large banner over the check-in counter. She'd mentioned to Dr. Matt Muller she was coming but wouldn't be staying. He and her dad had been good friends, but she never imagined Matt would do something like this.

When she looked behind the counter, the receptionist stood and started clapping. Others came from the back and joined in. Heat flamed Lydia's cheeks. She waved her arms. "Thanks. I'd planned on sneaking in, but this beats that idea."

Matt opened the door to the hallway that led to the exam rooms and entered the reception area. "That's what I figured. We couldn't let you do that without letting you know how happy we are that you survived."

Her assistant, JoAnn, followed him. "We all pitched in and brought goodies. The Lord was watching out for you. That's something to celebrate."

"Hear! Hear!" someone shouted.

There was a time when Lydia hadn't thought God cared what happened to her, especially in those dark days when she'd lost her baby and realized Aaron wasn't really there for her, either. She went through the motions of worshipping the Lord, but she'd decided years ago He was too busy to listen to her prayers.

"Thank you. I'm not going to say you shouldn't have done this because I'm hoping JoAnn baked her cinnamon rolls."

Her assistant grinned and nodded. "We have everything set up in the break room. I even made you some to take home."

"Thank you! I'm going to check on Mitch, then we'll party."

"He's a trouper. He's going home today." Matt gave Lydia a hug. "And his partner, Officer Nichols, is getting better. We have a lot to celebrate."

Like Matt she'd become attached to the SAR dogs

and the K-9s that were partnered with a police officer. She'd enjoyed having Brutus last night. He was so
well trained that he even got along with Cheri, while
Charlie remained hidden under her bed, one of his favorite places.

"Who's taking Mitch until Jake Nichols gets out of
the hospital?" Lydia headed for the back where Mitch
would be.

"Jesse Hunt is coming to pick him up this morning
on his break. Brutus and Mitch have always gotten
along." Matt stepped to the side to allow Lydia into
the large room with cages for the animals.

"This is the time I wish I had a fenced yard. I'd have
taken Mitch."

"You could walk him. He'll need the exercise. And
you can make sure he continues to progress."

Lydia opened the cage door as Mitch struggled to
stand. Before he hobbled two steps, she was next to
him, kneeling down and petting the tan-and-black German shepherd. As she checked him out, he nuzzled her.
"You're looking good, Mitch. Would you like to come
home with me?"

The dog barked.

"That's your answer," her partner said. "You should
talk with Jesse about taking Mitch."

"I think I will. I saw his SUV at the bistro. If he
hasn't come by here, I'll go see him when I leave." Having Mitch at her house would make Kate feel better—
and if she was honest with herself, she would, too.

Matt glanced at his watch. "Let's go eat. My first
appointment will be here in fifteen minutes."

"How's Dr. Stutsman fitting in?"

"He's not you. A bit set in his ways, but at least he

could help us while you're recuperating. He should be here soon."

"He's seventy and prefers camping and fishing now."

"Yeah, I know. That's all I hear about."

Closing the cage door, Lydia chuckled. "He reminds me of my father."

"Your dad was kind of set in his ways, too."

Lydia's chuckle evolved into laughter. "You think? *Change* was not in Dad's vocabulary."

"True. I guess you've spoiled me. I like going with the flow."

Lydia clasped Matt's shoulder. "You've made this transition easier."

At the break room, he paused. "Still want to leave after Kate graduates?"

She remembered telling him that when she'd met with him the first day. "I'm reconsidering."

"Good. I'm too old to go through breaking in another partner."

She studied the medium-sized man with salt-and-pepper hair and sharp eyes. "You're not old. You can't be a day over fifty."

"Fifty-four, and thank you for saying that." He indicated she go into the room first.

Lydia ate a bite from every dish brought and spent some time with the staff she'd come to care about. Maybe she could return earlier than she'd planned.

"I see the wheels turning in that mind of yours." JoAnn presented her with the leftover cinnamon rolls wrapped in aluminum foil to take home with her.

"I've only known you a year, and you think you can read my mind."

"I see the yearning on your face."

Lydia's gaze fixed on Dr. Stutsman, who had come in a few minutes ago. She leaned close to JoAnn and whispered, "Are you two getting along okay?"

Her assistant turned her back to the room full of staff. "Sure. I can get along with a grizzly."

"It's that bad?"

"Today's Friday. Aren't you coming back Monday?"

Lydia nodded.

"We're fine, but I've learned to appreciate you." JoAnn winked and pointed toward the door. "You look exhausted. Go home."

Lydia saluted. "Aye, aye." Then to everyone, she said, "Thank you so much for this party. I needed it after the week I've had. I'll be back on Monday." As the last word slipped from her mouth, she pictured a few days ago when the bomb exploded, and shuddered. So much had changed in that time. She would be glad when she returned to her normal routine.

She made her way toward the front entrance with her goodies. When she reached for the handle, the door opened, and she quickly stepped back. Jesse with Brutus beside him filled the entry.

"I saw your car. I thought I'd catch you to make sure Mitch will be okay to go home today." Dust covered Jesse's black uniform.

"Did you go Dumpster diving?"

One corner of his mouth hiked up. "Searching for clues can be a dirty job."

"I was coming to see you to give you and whoever else is working the site this." She thrust the foil-wrapped sweets into his hand. "JoAnn makes the best cinnamon rolls."

"Thanks." He stared at the gift for a few seconds, then looked her in the eye. "Is Mitch cleared to leave?"

"Yes, but I want to take him home."

"You think he might need a vet?"

"No, but Kate wasn't happy when I told her Brutus wasn't coming back tonight. Mitch is familiar with me. I've treated him several times this year, and best of all, I think Kate won't give me a hard time."

"But you don't have a fenced backyard."

"I think Kate will jump at the chance of walking him around out back. My little sis has taken after me as far as loving animals." *Not much else, though.*

"Are you sure you don't need Brutus?"

"Yes." She wanted to see more of Jesse, but she needed to remember it was only a case to him.

"Then that's fine with me. I'm so used to Brutus being around that it was lonely without him."

"Great. I'm going to load Mitch and some food into my car and take him home now. I need a long nap."

Instead of leaving, Jesse moved inside and shut the door. "Did you get any sleep last night? I was hoping Brutus would help you feel safe."

"He did. It was probably my four-hour nap yesterday that threw me off schedule." Although that could be part of the reason, the main one was the man standing in front of her. Even in a dusty police uniform, he commanded a person's full attention.

"And you're taking another one today?"

"Yep. You can carry the canned food."

After she showed him where it was kept, she took a leash and retrieved an excited Mitch from his cage. She adjusted her gait as the German shepherd adapted the way he walked with a missing back leg.

Out in the parking lot, Jesse set the food on the seat in back while Lydia helped the dog climb into the front seat of her gray Jeep. She shut the passenger door and came around the hood of the car.

"I thank you, and so does Kate, for letting us have Mitch."

Jesse peered at the bomb site and back to Lydia.

"Does Jake know about Mitch's leg?"

"No, I wanted him off the critical list and stabilized first. He was really attached to his dog."

She'd known that, but she had no choice if Mitch was to live. "I'd like to go with you when you tell him."

"You don't have to. I can break the news to him."

"It'll devastate him, but I feel I need to be the one. I made the decision and can explain the reason why Mitch lost his leg."

Jesse's barrier he kept between them fell in place. "I'll let Jake know now that he can receive visitors, then if you want you can talk to him."

Lydia slipped in behind the steering wheel, started the car and lowered her window. "Have you found anything helpful this morning?"

"Not yet, but every area has to be combed through."

While Lydia drove away from the animal hospital, she glanced at Jesse in the rearview mirror, his legs planted a foot apart, his gaze tracking her as she pulled out into traffic. She sighed as he disappeared from her sight. Probably a good thing. She didn't need to have a wreck, staring at him when she should be driving.

Jesse squatted next to Brutus and rubbed his hand down his back. "Break time is over. We have to get back to work. Sorry about your buddy not coming home with us."

As he rose and stretched, he thought about yesterday and spending more time with Lydia than he'd wanted. And yet, in the end, he didn't mind it because leaving Brutus with her and Kate felt like the right call. Even so, he'd stayed outside her house for an hour before leaving.

He couldn't shake what she'd told him about marrying Aaron. If he ever saw his high school friend, he'd throttle him. He'd known Aaron was a player and tried to warn her, but she'd refused to listen. If only she had... Would they have been together today? He'd asked himself that question quite a bit with conflicting answers each time. Now it was too late.

When he reached the bomb site, he picked up where he and Brutus had left off. Fifteen minutes into searching his section, his cell phone rang, his ring tone the call of a bull moose. He saw it was Thomas and asked, "I thought you were going to be at the bomb site. Has something happened?"

"Yes, but not another bomb. I got the autopsy information back on the waitress. She died from a large air embolism. After some investigation and looking at video feed, it has been ruled a murder. A medium-sized man was caught going into her room, dressed as an orderly, but no one on the staff fits his description. It turns out an orderly's badge was stolen in the locker room the day the waitress died."

"Then we have a photo of the guy."

"Sort of."

Jesse surveyed the area. "What do you mean?"

"It looks like a disguise, although we'll use the photo. Even if our bomber is using disguises, maybe this will help us. I'm just not sure how accurate it will be and the orderly had an uncanny way of avoiding the cameras. I can't find anyone he interacted with on the floor. I'm almost at the bomb site."

Jesse clicked off. If the waitress was murdered, then she must have seen something in the dining area or the bomber thought she did. What about Lydia? She couldn't remember, but the man wouldn't know that, and even if he did, he killed the waitress to get rid of a witness. Jesse tried calling Lydia on her cell phone, but she didn't answer. Spying Thomas's car pulling up, he hurried toward the detective.

Thomas met him partway. "I'm worried about Lydia. Did you just see her? Is she still at the animal hospital? I want to show her this picture."

"Yes and no. She's taking Mitch home with her. I'd feel a lot better about that if the dog wasn't injured. I tried calling her cell phone, but she isn't picking up. She wouldn't be home yet."

"Maybe she stopped somewhere. Doesn't have her cell. It died. We could be overreacting."

Jesse frowned. "I'd rather be overreacting than have something happen. I'm going to her house. I'll take the picture to show her."

"I'll have a patrol car near there go by Lydia's until you arrive. With this development, she needs police protection. Stay with her until I get everything set up. If this guy thought he needed to kill the waitress, then he must have thought she saw something. Lydia probably saw it, too."

"Yeah, let's hope she did. There's no guarantee." Jesse strode to his SUV and settled Brutus in the back. On the way he called her again, praying he was overreacting.

* * *

Lydia pulled into the driveway and punched a remote button to raise the garage door. "We're at my house, Mitch."

The German shepherd perked up on the seat beside her.

"I'm going to take the food in first. I'll be right back, then I'll show you my house. I have a couple of cats I need to put in the bathroom until you all are properly introduced."

Mitch cocked his head as though he understood every word she'd said. Dogs were attuned to a person's body language and tone of voice, so maybe he got the gist of it.

She rubbed the top of his head. "Then I'll take you for a walk out back."

Lydia slid from the backseat and grabbed the box of cans. When she lifted it, a pang of pain stabbed her chest. Her bruised ribs were healing but not fast enough for her. With the dog food in her arms, she fumbled to open the door into the house. When it swung wide, she almost fell through the entrance. She recovered her balance but not before the box crashed to the tile floor. Her actions only reinforced her earlier pain. She hurried to close the door to the garage before one of her cats got out and decided to investigate the strange dog in her car.

As she picked up the dog food that had rolled from the box, she began to have reservations about Mitch. She hadn't really thought about her two cats. Mitch could appease Kate but cause an animal war in the house.

One of the cans landed under her kitchen table. She

scooted a chair away and eased herself down to crawl after it. She grabbed it and backed out.

A sound caught her attention. Footsteps? The cats? Where were they? They were always in here greeting her when she returned home.

She rose slowly, her body already protesting the physical exertion. Her gaze swung from one end of the room to the other. Her cats weren't in the kitchen. She needed to find them to lock them up. It would take time to acclimate Charlie to Mitch. Cheri wouldn't have any trouble, so she would start with her.

Lydia headed for the dining room that flowed into the living room, calling their names. They usually came when she called, but occasionally they would ignore her. When she stopped in the foyer, she heard a cry coming from the hallway to the bedroom. She didn't want to leave Mitch alone in a new place for long, so she hurried toward the sound Cheri was making, like the cry of a baby.

The noise continued, emanating from her room at the end. As she approached, she tried to remember if she'd closed the door. Sometimes she did. She'd been rushing this morning and—

Her home phone rang.

The ringing of the phone cut through the silence. She gasped at the sudden sound and glanced over her shoulder. She froze. A man in a ski mask emerged from her bathroom. All she saw was the long knife in his hand.

SIX

Jesse disconnected his phone and stepped on the accelerator. She didn't even answer her house phone. Was she outside walking Mitch?

He was still ten minutes out, and he couldn't shake that something was wrong. What if the bomber followed her from the animal hospital and ran her off the road or…

He shook the what-ifs from his mind. It would only distract him from getting to Lydia. He took a sharp curve ten miles over the speed limit. At least Thomas had called for a patrol car to go to Lydia's. But what if there wasn't an officer available in the area?

He clenched his jaw, hoping to make her house in half the time.

Not taking her eyes off the knife in the man's hand, Lydia lunged for her bedroom door, shoved it open, whirled around and banged it shut. She threw the lock in place, then backed away.

Off to the side Cheri perched on her bed, wailing as though she was being assaulted. Something slammed against the door. The lock held. But not for long. The

wood wasn't thick. She went to her bedside table to re-
trieve her father's revolver. As her assailant attacked
the flimsy barrier, his pounding fist vied with her
heartbeat—ever increasing. Although the weapon was
always loaded, she checked to see if the gun had bullets in every chamber. Empty! The spare ammunition
was kept in a hall closet.

Her cell was in the car. Why wasn't there an exten-
sion of the home phone in here? She frantically looked
around for any kind of weapon to use. Nothing use-
ful against a knife. Her gaze fell on the window at the
end of her bed. Maybe if she could climb out of it and
escape…

A crashing sound, as if the intruder was throwing
his body against the door, rattled the pictures on the
wall nearby. She rushed to the window and fought to
unlock it. It wouldn't budge. After wiping her sweaty
hands on her jeans, she poured all her strength into
trying one last time before she searched for something
to break the glass. The bolt gave way, and she shoved
the window up.

The sound of sirens—not far away—echoed in the
air. Suddenly an eerie silence came from the hallway.
What was the intruder doing? Looking for something
else to smash the door open? Either way she had to
get out of her bedroom. The sirens probably weren't
for her.

She poked her head out to see how far down she
would have to jump to the ground. A motion out of the
corner of her eye caught her attention. A man dressed
in black jeans and T-shirt ran across her yard from her
back door, heading for the woods nearby. It had to be
her attacker, although earlier she hadn't even noticed

what he was wearing. Or could there be two people and the other one was waiting out in the hallway for her?

Jesse turned the corner onto the road that ran in front of Lydia's home. He spied a patrol car parked in front with the lights flashing. As he shut down his emotions, preparing himself to handle anything coming his way, he pulled up behind the cruiser and glanced toward her house.

Lydia came out onto the porch with Officer Williams, her arms crisscrossed over her chest. The look on her face twisted his heart. Something happened there, but at least she was alive.

He climbed from his white SUV and rounded the rear to release Brutus. He strode toward Lydia, and her head swiveled toward him. She bit her lip, then returned her attention to Officer Williams.

"What happened?" Jesse asked as he approached them.

"Dr. McKenzie found a man in her house. I was going to have her sit in my car while I take a look inside."

"He's gone. He ran out the back door toward the woods." Lydia's voice quavered, and she clamped her lips together.

Jesse headed for the left side of her house. "How long ago?"

"Four or five minutes ago," the police officer answered.

"Stay here and guard her. Brutus and I will follow the intruder's trail. Don't leave her alone."

Officer Williams nodded his head.

Jesse disappeared from their view, hurrying his

steps. He wanted to catch this man—put an end to the past weeks' terror. Brutus picked up a scent at the back door, and Jesse gave him a long leash as they charged across the yard into the woods. His partner weaved through the trees as though the intruder wasn't sure which way to go. Good. Maybe he had a chance to catch the guy even with his lead.

In the thick brush to the left, a flash of black caught Jesse's attention. He turned Brutus loose, and his dog made a beeline toward the heavy foliage a couple of football fields to the west. The sound of a motorcycle's engine revving spurred Jesse on faster. When he broke out of the line of trees onto a path, his K-9 raced down the trail after a person in black hunkered over a motorcycle speeding around a curve.

Jesse ran twenty yards behind his Rottweiler and rounded the turn onto a paved road. Brutus and the motorcycle had disappeared from view.

So cold. Lydia sank onto a chair on her front porch, her whole body shaking, and massaged her hands up and down her arms.

Leaning against the house, Officer Williams stood next to her, panning the yard. "Can you remember anything about the guy in your house?"

"I wish I could give you a description of the man in the hallway. I just don't remember anything other than the knife he had."

"But you think it was a man?"

Yeah, she did—even before she glimpsed the person running away from her house. She tried to recall anything to help catch the intruder. Did he have on jeans, a black T-shirt? Although she only stared at the knife, it was against a dark background. "Yes."

"Okay, you said the guy running from the house was medium height and build. How about his hair color?"

She'd given the officer a brief description right when he showed up, thinking he might go after the intruder, but he'd told her Detective Caldwell had insisted he stay with her. She visualized in her mind the man escaping toward the woods. "He had on a black ball cap, and dark brown hair was sticking out of the back."

"Then dark brown hair, medium height. At least it's a start."

One that fit a lot of men in Anchorage. Why didn't she think to study the guy? Because she was too busy trying to get away from him. "Is Detective Caldwell coming here?" she asked, glad that at least Kate had been at school.

"I don't know."

Lydia looked toward the left, wondering where Jesse was. He knew how to protect himself, but this man— if he was the bomber—had nothing to lose by killing him. Or her.

She clasped her hands together in her lap, squeezing so tightly her knuckles whitened. She checked her watch. Jesse had been gone fifteen *long* minutes. What if the intruder hid and then attacked him? No, he'd be all right. Brutus, too. They worked well together.

Lord, I haven't asked for much, but please keep Jesse and Brutus safe.

The prayer came to her mind unexpectedly. She hadn't prayed much in the past years. She'd given up when hers went unanswered after her daughter died.

Finally, five minutes later, Jesse came around the

side of the house with Brutus but no intruder. She sank against the back of the chair and unclasped her hands. He was unhurt. But the man was still out there.

Jesse mounted the steps. His look zeroed in on her. "Are you okay?"

She started to nod, but she couldn't. She wasn't all right. A huge knot twisted her stomach. Her ribs were sore, and finally she was beginning to realize how close she had come to being hurt or killed. Again. The trembling sped through her body, and there was nothing she could do to stop it.

"Officer Williams, why don't you walk through the house? See how the man got inside."

Her head lowered, she heard the screen door bang closed. She sensed Jesse moving toward her, but for the life of her, she couldn't look at him. If she did, she might totally fall apart, and she couldn't. It wouldn't change anything.

Jesse squatted in front of her and laid his hands over hers.

She finally looked into his eyes. The kindness in them battered at the dam she desperately tried to shore up. They weren't even friends anymore. All she was to Jesse was a possible witness to a crime…one who couldn't even remember anything to help the police—to help herself.

He cradled her hands between his as though he cared. His gaze softened, and for a few seconds, she was swept back to when they had been dating and she'd fallen while skiing. He'd been there by her side almost instantly, holding her like this and asking her if she was okay.

She slid her eyes closed before the emotions cramming her throat turned to tears and demanded release.

"Lydia, I'm not going to let anything happen to you. Thomas is going to move you to a safe house, and you'll have a guard with you at all times. That's what he's working on right now."

She coated her dry throat and asked, "How did you know what was going on? If the officer hadn't turned on his siren and arrived when he did…" The sounds of the intruder attacking her door echoed through her mind as though it were still happening. She flinched with each strike.

Jesse released her hands and drew her to her feet, then wrapped his arms around her. "We now believe the waitress was murdered. When I was told about the autopsy report, I headed here while Thomas dispatched a patrol car in the area."

"If the officer had been five minutes later, the intruder would have gotten into my bedroom. My gun wasn't loaded. It should have been." She pulled back from Jesse. "I never unloaded it. Dad had it there, and I kept it in the same place."

"Would Kate have?"

"I'll ask her, but I don't think so. She doesn't like guns, and when Dad tried to teach her to shoot, she refused. But she never had a problem with me having it for protection. She just didn't want to be the one holding it."

Jesse glanced around. "Let's go inside. I see a few of your neighbors are getting curious." With his arm around her shoulder, he walked with her into the foyer. "When you feel ready, I want you to tell me and show me what you did when you came home."

Lydia cupped her hand over her mouth. "Oh, no. Mitch is still out in my car in the garage." She hurried toward the kitchen and almost ran into Officer Williams coming out of the room. She could vaguely hear Jesse talking to the police officer as she entered the garage.

When she opened the door, Mitch perked up and slowly climbed down. "I'm sorry it took so long." She petted him, glad he hadn't been with her. He might have gotten hurt further trying to apprehend the intruder.

The German shepherd was learning how to compensate for his lost leg. The K-9s she treated were always very smart dogs and able to adapt to different kinds of situations they found themselves in. He followed her into the house. His tail began to wag when he spied Brutus near Jesse.

"Where's Officer Williams?"

"Checking the perimeter. We haven't figured out how the man got into the house."

"You think he had a key?"

"I don't know. If so, how did he get it?"

Which also brought up the question why did he kill the waitress at the hospital but not her? He didn't try until now. "If he's trying to kill me, why now and not at the hospital?"

"Several reasons possibly. You had people in your room coming and going all the time. Kate. Bree. Me. Your assistant from work. The waitress didn't have any family nearby. She'd recently moved to Alaska. Usually it was just staff moving in and out of her room. If he impersonated an orderly, he could find enough time when no one else was around."

"Do you have a photo of the man you think did it?"

"Yes, a couple, but not any good ones." Jesse opened his cell phone and showed her the ones Thomas sent him from the surveillance cameras at the hospital. "I know that part of his face is hidden, but does this trigger anything? Was it the man you saw today?"

She stared at the pictures—one with the left side of his face while the other was a full-body shot; but in the distance and not clear. "This guy has blond hair so that's different from the intruder."

"Hair color can be changed."

"It's hard to tell for sure. His build seems familiar if I use the door as a reference point for height, but he's chubby around the waist. I don't think the guy in my house was." But uncertainty nagged her. Was she trying to fill in details because she wanted to remember? Was she missing something? She thought back to the visitors and staff who were in her hospital room and…

Jesse started to take his cell phone back.

"Wait." She clasped his wrist to still his movements. "I remember seeing a guy like this in my room. Bree had me walking in the corridor, and when we came back into the room, he was there. He said he had just finished changing my sheets and he rushed out. So many staff came and went, I really didn't think about it, even though he struck me as a little weird. You know how it is in a hospital. The parade of people through your room makes it difficult to get much rest."

"That's why I avoid hospitals as much as possible."

"Have you ever had to stay in one?"

"Only twice in the ER. They almost admitted me the time I was shot, but I managed to avoid it."

"You were shot? On the job?"

"Yes. It wasn't that big of a deal. Hardly more than a flesh wound."

There was so much she didn't know about Jesse now. And there was much he didn't know about her. They were strangers in many ways, and that thought saddened her.

After Lydia put some water down for Mitch and Brutus, Jesse said, "Tell me what happened once you came inside the house."

She went through the steps she'd taken earlier. "Cheri was carrying on, and I was following her cries and looking for where Charlie was. Neither one came to greet me." She paused. "Wait. Where is Charlie? Cheri had been shut up in my bedroom." She surveyed the hallway and began checking the rooms—the third bedroom that her dad had turned into an office, the bathroom, Kate's room and then she came to hers, the master bedroom, with the door nearly destroyed. It drove home how close she'd come to being killed. "Cheri was on my pillow. When the pounding started, she went under the bed."

Lydia knelt on the floor and peeked under it. Two sets of eyes stared at her from the dimness. "Charlie is with Cheri. I didn't put them in the bedroom. The intruder must have." She pulled Cheri out and Charlie followed until he spied Jesse with Brutus and then he dashed out of the room.

Lydia rose with Cheri in her arms and sank onto her bed. "Thank God he didn't kill them. I don't know what…" Her voice quavered, making the rest of the sentence difficult to finish. She hugged Cheri against her, her eyes watering. What could have happened hit her like an avalanche, and this time she couldn't contain the emotions overwhelming her.

Jesse sat next to her, his side pressed against hers as though to let her know he was there for her. She wasn't alone. She buried her face in Cheri's long fur as she struggled to stop the tears slipping down her cheeks. She appreciated Jesse's silence because he knew how she felt about crying in front of others. She'd always fought not to, even when she attended her father's funeral and Kate had bawled in her arms. As the older sibling with a grieving father, Lydia had learned to shut her sorrow down quickly after her mother left.

Cheri's purrs calmed her, and she drew in deep breaths to compose herself. "I start thinking about what could have happened to my animals or Mitch if circumstances had been different."

"And you. I want you to pack your clothes. After Officer Williams checks the perimeter, he's going to pick up Kate from school a little early. I'll need you to call the school and let them know. Then she'll need to pack, and we'll get out of here. I'm not sure they'll find anything, but I'm going to have the crime scene techs here to check. Do you remember if he had on gloves?"

The vision of the knife in the intruder's hand materialized in her mind. "Yes, black ones. Not thick winter ones."

"I'll still have them go through and take latent prints where they can." His gaze latched on to the revolver on the bedside table. "Also go over the gun. See if there are other prints beside yours on it. And if he was here before you came home from the hospital maybe he left something or took something that would give us a clue."

"So you think he took the bullets?"

"Unless Kate did. Probably."

"I'll ask Kate about that, but I don't think she'd have done it."

"Which means you might have had an intruder before today who went through your possessions."

So she hadn't overreacted. "Why?"

"I can only speculate." Jesse twisted toward her and framed her face with his large hands. "Why would he be going around bombing different places in Anchorage? Or, why would he go through your belongings? Maybe to get a sense of you. We may never know. Not all people think in a normal, logical way. Their reasoning won't make sense to us."

"Is there any way the person in my house was a robber and had nothing to do with the bombings?"

"Have there been any break-ins around here?"

"Not that I've heard of."

"It's possible, but usually when they break in, we can tell. This person didn't. We need to proceed as if the guy behind the bombings either came himself or sent someone."

"To kill me," she finally said aloud.

Frowning, Jesse nodded.

A shudder rippled down her body. "Then I'd better remember what he thinks I know. Somehow I must have seen him, but there were a lot of people there that day in the bistro, coming and going."

"You will."

"How can you say that? You don't know for sure."

"Yes, I do. I've been praying you will."

She twisted around, leaning back as she looked at

Jesse. "When you were in high school, you never went to church. What happened?"

"I blame Thomas. After you left, he dragged me to his church. At first I didn't pay much attention to what Pastor Paul was saying, but slowly the words began to sink in. My faith has helped me make sense of all the evil I see in this world. If I didn't have the Lord to fall back on, I'm not sure I could be a police officer."

"And I did the opposite. I went to church all the time here, but when I left Anchorage, I grew further away from my faith. After losing my baby and Aaron's betrayal, I was struggling just to get through each day. Working a full-time job and going to college took all my time. I'd come home and collapse on the bed."

"I'm sorry you went through that."

She tilted her head to the side and tried to read the true meaning behind those words. "Do you really feel that way? You have every right to say, you made your bed and now you have to sleep in it."

Jesse looked away from her. "I'm not going to tell you I wasn't angry. I was. I felt betrayed. It took a long time to get beyond those feelings."

"I'm sorry." She touched his arm, needing the tactile contact with him.

"You should come to church. Pastor Paul is such an inspiration."

"I might, but wasn't your church the one that was bombed?"

"Yes, but that won't stop Pastor Paul. We'll have service in the part that still remains. If you want I'll take you this Sunday."

The invitation took her by surprise—a reversal of roles from when they were teenagers. "I'd like that."

"Good."

His smile warmed her and gave her a seed of hope that they would at least become friends again. "You never said what happened when you and Brutus went after the intruder. Did Brutus find his scent?"

"Yes, but we were a minute or so too late. I saw a man dressed in a black T-shirt and jeans riding away on a motorcycle. I only got a glimpse before he went around a curve on the trail in the woods. Brutus went after him, but the intruder had a good head start. I ran after Brutus and had to call him back. I think he would have raced after the bike until he dropped."

"Sounds like you had a good workout."

"You could say that." Jesse pushed off the bed and faced her. "I'm walking through the house with Brutus while you pack. Don't forget to call the school. Williams should be through and on his way to pick up Kate."

Lydia watched the pair walk from her room with Cheri hot on their trail. She was a busybody, always wanting to know what everyone was doing in the house while Charlie hid.

After calling the school, she retrieved a piece of luggage and began filling it with clothes. She wanted to take her dad's gun, and she needed some ammunition, which was in the hall closet. The door was ajar—no doubt Charlie's handiwork. He was a master at opening them if they weren't totally latched. As she swung it wide, Charlie darted out of another one of his favorite hiding places and charged toward the living room.

As she reached for the box of ammo on the top shelf, a loud crash filled the air.

SEVEN

Charlie raced from the living room and down the hallway. Lydia grabbed the box of ammunition, then strode to the entrance of the room, almost afraid to see what happened. A ceramic lamp lay on the wooden floor, shattered into several pieces. Mitch sat by the mess with Cheri next to him. Jesse came from the dining area with Brutus.

Jesse kneaded his nape. "Maybe I should have left Mitch in the kitchen, but Cheri kept whining and scratching on the door. I gave in when Mitch began whining, too."

"Who did this? Did you see?" Lydia moved toward the busted lamp.

"Charlie. I think Mitch was trying to be friendly and Charlie jumped up on the table to get away." Jesse joined her and stooped to pick up the pieces.

"He tries to go to high ground."

When Jesse reached for a second shard, his hand paused for a few seconds. "Here take this one." He passed her the first chunk, then took the second one and examined it. "This is a bug. And not the kind that crawl around."

Lydia stared at the small device on the underside of the lamp, too shocked to say anything.

"I'll get a bug detector out here and see if there are more. Do you have a paper sack?"

She nodded and hurried into the kitchen to grab one.

When she returned, Jesse had on latex gloves. He carefully put the sections of the lamp into the bag. "There might be latent prints on this that aren't mine or yours."

The events of the day caught up with her. She collapsed on the couch nearby, trying to assimilate what was going on. It had been bad enough an intruder was in her house, but to have someone listening to what she had said unnerved her even more. "If Charlie hadn't knocked it over, we would never have known."

Jesse set the sack on the coffee table and sat next to Lydia. "The crime scene techs would probably have found it."

"When will they be here?"

"Half an hour. Kate should be here soon, then we'll leave when they show up."

"Will Kate be allowed to go to school?"

Jesse rose and pulled her to her feet and headed for the porch. "We don't know how many bugs he planted or where."

"I didn't think about that."

"To answer your question, Kate isn't the target. I'll discuss it with Thomas, and if he thinks it's okay, I don't see why not. Over the years schools have become more secure because of school shootings." He cocked a grin. "And I have a feeling Kate wouldn't want to be locked in a house indefinitely. She'll have to have an escort, though, to and from."

"Where will we be?"

"My house. I told Thomas if I'm going to be the lead on your detail I want a place I know has a top-notch alarm system and neighbors who are vigilant. Several other police officers live on my street."

"You're the lead on my detail? You didn't even want me to call you a few days ago if I remember correctly."

"Can't a guy change his mind?"

"Well, yes, but—"

Officer Williams pulled into the driveway. Kate stalked toward them, zeroed in on Lydia and headed for her with Officer Williams right behind her. The poor man must have gotten an earful because Lydia knew that thunderous look on Kate's face.

Kate tossed her backpack onto a porch chair. "We're leaving here? Why?"

Stay calm. Losing my temper won't make the situation any better. "Because someone was in our house today when I returned home from the animal hospital. He had a knife, but I managed to get into my bedroom and lock the door." Lydia slanted a look at Jesse. "The autopsy of the waitress indicates she was murdered. Jesse was already on his way here, and Thomas dispatched a patrol car until Jesse could arrive. If they hadn't, I don't know what would have happened." Her voice remained even, but her stomach roiled and the muscles in her back and neck tensed as she thought of her near miss.

Color drained from her sister's face, and her mouth hung open. "In our house? How?"

"We think he had a key. Where is yours?" Jesse rose from the couch.

Kate moved to her backpack and dug into a side

pocket, then held the key up. "It's a new lock. We haven't had these long."

Lydia shoved to her feet and closed the space between her and Kate. "There's a chance he had access to the one that Bree brought me at the hospital."

"But you had yours when you came home."

"He could have had it copied." Jesse indicated for Officer Williams to follow him.

When they were gone, Lydia faced Kate. "I don't like this any more than you do. You'll be escorted to and from school until this guy is found."

Kate stomped toward the front door and went inside. "You're kidding! When can I see Connor?"

"Never" almost slipped from Lydia's mouth, but she knew that would make the teen even more attractive to Kate. She followed her sister into the house. "We'll see. I'll have to talk to Jesse about that, but in the meantime, don't let anyone know where we're staying. If someone asks you, just say a safe house."

Kate huffed. "I didn't even witness anything. I'm not the one the bomber is after. Why am I being restricted?"

"Because I would worry. We don't know what this maniac is thinking. By what he's done so far, he certainly isn't rational and sane." She didn't care if he'd bugged her house and heard what she thought about him.

"Go on TV and make a statement that you have no memory of the bombing. Then he'll leave you alone."

"Again, we don't know that." Lydia wanted to hug her sister. In all her bluster, she could tell Kate was worried, because she was twirling her long, sandy-colored hair. She did that when she was nervous or upset. "We can talk more after we move. You need to pack a bag. I'll feel better when we're at…our safe place." She surveyed the living room, her gaze pausing on where the lamp had been. She wasn't sure she ever wanted to come back even after the man was caught. He was in her house, possibly twice, and obviously got in easily.

"Okay." Kate started to turn toward the foyer, stopped and swung back around. She threw her arms around Lydia, then hurried toward her room.

The hug brought tears to Lydia's eyes and gave her hope that somehow their sisterly bond could be renewed. Their relationship had been strained, especially ever since Connor came into Kate's life three months ago.

Later that evening, Thomas sat with Lydia and Jesse at Jesse's kitchen table while Lydia's sister was in the bedroom they shared, probably video-chatting with Connor. The other police officer who would be guarding them through the night would be arriving in the next hour.

"So how is this going to work?" Lydia shifted her attention from Jesse to Thomas. "I'm going to have to tell Kate something. Thankfully other than that initial outburst, she has been quiet. I told her she would be escorted to and from school, but otherwise she needed to be here. She wasn't happy about that. She wanted to know how she was going to see Connor."

"Young love. They tend to have tunnel vision when it comes to each other. All they want is to be together, no matter what." Thomas put his notepad on the table.

"You've described Kate and Connor's relationship

accurately. But she'll get to see him at least at school."
Lydia could remember how she'd felt about Jesse when
she was her sister's age. She'd always wanted to be
with him. Those feelings could be intense, whether
they lasted or not.

Thomas's lips set in a tight line. "I do have one
stipulation. Since tomorrow is Saturday, I'll be meeting with the principal and going through their security
precautions. I know they have more in place since the
second bomb went off. But Kate will have to agree to
have the officer escort her to and from the building."

"She won't like that. Is it possible to have a young
female officer and not have her dressed in a uniform?"
Lydia could already imagine what Kate would say.

"That can be arranged, but I like the idea of a uni-
formed cop with you at all times. I want to make this
as painless as possible, but I want that guy to know
you are being protected. If you go to work, there'll be
two with you. The person taking Kate to school will
join you at the animal hospital and be in the reception
area. All outside doors except the main one will be
locked, and you'll also have a police officer by your
side at all times."

"Even when I operate on an animal?"

Thomas nodded.

"Who?" Lydia looked toward Jesse. "You?"

"No, I'm going to be investigating the case while
you're at work, then take over after that. We're doing
two twelve-hour shifts."

"When are you going to sleep?"

Jesse's golden-brown gaze gleamed, totally directed
at her as if Thomas weren't even in the room. "Don't
worry. I'll get my sleep. The department can only spare

four officers right now. Although the cooks haven't been threatened like you, we have to give them protection, too. The bombings have really taxed our resources. We're asking for some help from the state police because I'd like to have two-person teams on eight-hour shifts. I'm hoping one of them is Chance O'Malley. You're familiar with him since he's involved in search and rescue. Hopefully that can be arranged by the time you go to work on Monday."

She was *not* going to melt at that look that made her feel so special. In high school he'd do that in the one class they'd shared. She didn't even know how she made an A in the subject. "Good. The more people I know around me the better."

"You're taking this awfully calm," Thomas interjected.

"You should have seen me when Officer Williams and Jesse first showed up. There was nothing calm about me. Will Officer Williams be one of my guards?"

"Yes. He requested it." Thomas leaned forward and looked at his pad. "Here's what we know. The fragments of the bomb found at the bistro are similar to the other two that went off at the church and hardware store. C-4 plastic explosives were used, but the one difference between the first two and the bistro is the amount. The bomb was more powerful at the bistro."

"We finally have an array of photos of all the victims," Jesse said. "We thought if you take a look at them, you might remember something—someone you saw who isn't among the pictures. Then you can describe the person to our artist. We have some other leads that we're developing into sketches. Bree is doing what she can. We're trying to track down people who left before the bomb went off."

Lydia closed her eyes and tried to visualize the bistro before she went to the restroom. Who was there? Anyone who left at that time? But all she saw was Melinda's look when the laughing track sounded. She couldn't seem to get past that. "I'll do what I can, but I don't know if I'm ever going to be a help to you."

Jesse began lining up the photos of the victims on the table. "Relax. If you can't, then you can't. Look at each one. Do you remember seeing them?"

Relax? The first picture she homed in on was of Melinda, smiling as she so often did while greeting customers. Everything else vanished. Her vision blurred, and she looked away. Flashes of the explosion like a strobe light raced through her mind.

Jesse put his hand over hers. "It's okay. You take all the time you need. If you want, we can do this tomorrow morning before we go see Jake at the hospital."

"You two are going to see him?" Thomas asked.

Until he had said that, Lydia again felt just she and Jesse were the only two in the room. His comforting touch centered her in the here and now. "Yes, now that he's stable, I want to take Mitch so he can see he'll be all right."

"Good. He needs something to cheer him up. I know what a special bond an officer and his K-9 develop." Thomas closed his notepad. "We have a few leads we're running down, Lydia. You aren't the only one. The C-4 is homemade so we're looking at the ingredients and places that sell them. We're going through all the videos at the hospital, trying to find a better photo of the orderly. We're looking for a vehicle that might have been the getaway car from the last bomb site."

"When is Melinda's funeral?" Lydia needed to say goodbye to her friend.

"The family is planning a memorial service at the end of next week. We're going to be there filming it to see if people who go are on some of the surveillance tapes we have." Thomas rose. "But we're hoping we catch the guy before that."

Lydia latched on to Melinda's photo again. "I need to go to the service."

"I think it'll be all right. They're holding it at a park, and we're covering each service for the victims, even staking the place out beforehand and having a bomb dog go through before it starts. Now, I'd better go. I know it's been a long day for you."

Lydia started to stand, but Jesse clasped her shoulder. "I'll see Thomas out and be right back."

While she waited for Jesse to return, she picked up the nearest picture and studied it. She knew the woman. She was one of the regulars. By the time he came into the kitchen and refreshed his coffee, she'd singled out a few more familiar faces, all regulars like the woman.

"Would you like another cup of tea?" Jesse placed his mug on the table.

She shook her head.

He sat next to her. "Who are these people?"

"The ones I don't know or remember seeing." She waved toward the group segregated off to the side. "These people I know, but honestly I don't necessarily remember them there that day except for Melinda." She stared into his warm, kind eyes. "What's wrong with me? I should be able to identify more than Melinda."

"When you go through a trauma, you often shut the incident out. You don't want to relive it."

"No, but I've been trying. I need to. The more I think about it, I believe I saw something." Lydia massaged her temples. "But my mind isn't cooperating."

"I know a therapist you might talk to. She works with trauma victims."

"Please. I have to do something. I don't want to live my life in fear that this guy is going to come after me."

"He isn't if I can do anything to stop him." Jesse took a sip of his coffee. "Thomas wants me to tell you what the crime scene techs found at your house. He got the report right before coming over."

"Why didn't he say anything?"

Jesse gathered up the photos. "He didn't want to overwhelm you all at once, but I know you're tough and would rather know everything we know."

"This doesn't sound good."

"There were several listening devices in your house—in the kitchen, your bedroom and of course, the living room, but there was also two cameras found. One in the living room and the other in your bedroom."

Stunned, Lydia stared at Jesse, but no thoughts came into her head for a long moment. She opened her mouth to reply but snapped it close. She sagged back in her chair.

"We're doing everything we can to track where the surveillance equipment came from." Worry knitted his forehead.

Slowly, Lydia began to process his words. She released a long breath. "Listening devices are one thing, but cameras give me a chill." Goose bumps covered her whole body, and she rubbed her hands up and down her arms. "Why the cameras?"

Jesse shrugged. "Covering all his bases. I think I know why he came after you. Remember when we talked last night in the kitchen?"

She nodded. "He didn't want to take the chance I'd remember something because I certainly was determined enough. So that's why he came to my house before I was let out of the hospital. It was hard to get to me there so he wanted to keep track of what I was remembering."

"If we'd only known, we could have set a trap for him."

"I'm willing to be bait if it will put an end to this."

"No! That wasn't what I meant. I won't risk your life like that." Jesse's mouth firmed to a hard, straight line.

"Then how do we end this?"

"By investigating, looking for any kind of connection between the hardware store, the church and the bistro. I've been digging into that aspect. We think it's random and it might be, but what if it isn't? I've been working with Pastor Paul about the parishioners, newcomers and visitors. We have to look at all possibilities."

"Because the bomber is escalating and he'll probably hit another target soon?"

"Yes, and we have no idea whether it's random or connected. We're cross-checking people associated with the hardware store and my church. It will be harder with the bistro because the owner was killed and her records were destroyed."

Massaging her temples, she needed to change the subject. "Are Mitch and Brutus still outside?"

"Yes. I'm leaving Brutus in the backyard during the night. He has a doghouse. I'll bring Mitch inside. He may have only three legs, but he is a well-trained K-9. Between them we should be alerted if anyone comes here."

"And your alarm system will help, too. I'm going to have to invest in one, although I don't know if I can go back to that house."

"Give it time."

She and Kate grew up in that home, but the bomber had spoiled it for her, and she wouldn't be surprised if her sister didn't want to return, either. She had good memories there until her mother abandoned them when Kate was three months. Everything changed after that, but at least at that time Jesse was a big part of her life.

"Maybe you should get a dog, too. I can help you find a good guard dog."

"I'm not sure after what happened earlier with Charlie and Mitch. He isn't a social animal. At least he gets along with Cheri."

"It's still something you might want to consider. Animals do adapt over time, especially when things settle down."

"What's that?" Lydia chuckled. "Charlie needs stability. Both of them are going to start thinking I abandoned them. But with them back at the animal hospital, at least I can see them during the day. I'm hoping that will help him because I'd hate to split Cheri and Charlie up. He does respond to her, but then they've been together since they were born."

Jesse rose. "I'll get Mitch. I've set up a place for him in the bedroom you're sharing with Kate."

"You don't want him able to roam your house? Or, are you putting him with us to make us feel safe?"

"That's part of the reason. But the night detail will take care of making sure the house isn't breached." Jesse stepped outside for a minute and called the dogs.

Lydia took Jesse's and her mug to the sink and rinsed them out. She liked his house. The comfortable furniture invited a person to relax. The walls were painted beige with photographs of different places in Alaska hanging up. Did Jesse take the breathtaking pictures? He used to love photography when they were teenagers.

She moved into the great room with a large stone fireplace and her gaze immediately fell on a photo in a wooden frame over the black leather couch. It was of a mountain at sunset, and the play of colors on the snow-covered terrain dazzled her with its brilliance. Whoever took it had to have been on a taller mountain looking down on the scene.

"I took that last winter when Chance, David and I went mountain climbing."

She gasped and swung toward him standing in the entrance to the room with Mitch beside him. "I didn't hear you. I was too engrossed in the picture. Did you take all the ones hanging in your house?"

"Yes. I'd rather be shooting with my camera than my gun, although I always take one with me in the wilderness for protection."

"Then why did you decide to be a police officer?"

"Because I wanted to help protect people. When I was twenty and attending a community college, there was a male student who came on campus with a gun, shooting people at random. There were four of us hiding in a room as he went through the building. I knew I was in God's hands, but the other three were freaking out. I was there that day to keep them calm and quiet. The shooter didn't find us. After that day, I wanted to help others feel safe, not helpless."

What else had Jesse gone through since they parted? That incident shaped his future like her failed marriage to Aaron had changed her and made her more determined to do what she'd always dreamed of— becoming a veterinarian. Her father and she had become estranged because of her relationship with Aaron, but she'd still wanted to follow in her father's steps, even if he never knew or cared.

"Well, this person—" she pointed to herself "—feels that way right now. Thank you." She held her breath, hoping he wouldn't say it was his job.

"I'm glad you feel that way."

Enjoying this subtle change in their relationship, Lydia started to ask him about the photograph of a mother polar bear with her cub, but the doorbell rang.

"That must be Officer Collins, the other half of the nightshift." As he strolled into the foyer, he put his hand on his gun in its holster at his waist.

That action underscored the danger she was in.

When the tall female officer came into the living room, Lydia shook her hand and said, "Thank you for being here, Officer Collins."

She grinned. "Please call me Mary. I want to do my part to bring this bomber to justice."

"I'll give you the grand tour and we'll discuss duties," Jesse said.

"I'm Lydia, and that's my cue to go to bed. It's been a *long* day."

"Yeah, I heard what happened at your house. I won't let it happen on my watch." Mary petted Mitch before following Jesse into the kitchen.

Lydia made her way to the master bedroom with Mitch by her side. This was Jesse's room, but he had insisted that she and Kate stay in it because of its large size and the private bathroom. When she entered, Kate sat on the king-size bed working on a school project on her laptop.

Her sister looked up. "Who was at the door?"

"Officer Mary Collins, the other one staying to-night." Lydia shut the door after Mitch hobbled into the room, spied a bed on the floor next to the bedside table and settled down on the large pillow. "Mitch is sleeping in here."

"Good. What's gonna happen to him? He can't be a K-9 dog anymore." Kate closed her laptop.

"He'll be retired. It's possible his partner will keep him."

"Even if a new K-9 is assigned to him?"

"Sure. You see how well Brutus and Mitch get along."

"If he doesn't want him, can we have him?"

Kate's question reminded Lydia of Jesse's sugges-tion about a guard dog. "That's definitely something to consider, but Jake is attached to Mitch so maybe we'll need to think of getting a different dog."

"Good. We agree on something." Kate glanced at her cell phone, then back at Lydia. "Can Connor come over tomorrow?"

Her first instinct was to say no, but her disapproval of the teen wasn't changing Kate's mind. She would leave the decision up to Jesse. "You need to run it by

Jesse. This is his house, and he's in charge of the officers protecting us. Did you tell Connor where we are?"

Kate stared at her lap. "No, you told me not to tell anyone."

"Kate?"

Her sister looked right at Lydia. "Really, I didn't."

"Okay." Lydia took her pajamas out of the drawer Jesse emptied so they had a place for their clothing. "I'm going to bed. I'm exhausted." She started for the bathroom.

"I told him. It just came out. I didn't mean to."

Kate's words rushed out of her mouth so fast it took Lydia a moment to digest what she'd said. Lydia turned toward her sister. "Then you'll need to tell Jesse that, too, but thank you for telling me the truth."

"Connor won't tell anyone. He loves me." Kate's upper teeth dug into her lower lip.

"You've only known him three months. It takes—"

"I'm seventeen. I know what I want and what I need. Do you? You certainly made a mess of your life at my age, so I'm not so sure you're the one to give me any advice."

"Because I made mistakes at your age, I know some pitfalls I hope you don't fall into."

"You're not me." Kate's glare drilled into Lydia.

Without another word, Lydia pivoted and marched into the bathroom, closing the door. She sank onto the tub's edge and stared at herself in the mirror, her hands gripping the cold ledge. How was she going to bridge the rift with Kate?

Lord, it's me again. What am I doing wrong? Why is my life falling apart around me? I feel paralyzed. Abandoned. First Mom left, then Dad and even Aaron. I can't go through that again. Please don't abandon me, too.

EIGHT

"I think that's what he looked like." Lydia studied the sketch the police artist drew from her description of the orderly in her hospital room. "I really didn't pay much attention, and he didn't stay long at all. I only saw him that one time."

The artist pulled out another drawing. "This is what Dr. Stone described."

Lydia swung her attention between the two pictures of a man with medium-length blond hair, a mustache and closely set dark eyes. "They're similar, so hopefully that'll help your case." Lydia glanced over her shoulder at Jesse. "Does that fit anyone who works at the hospital?"

"No. After I got Bree's sketch, I checked. The man in your room wasn't an orderly."

The sketch artist closed his pad and stood. "If you need me again, call. I want this guy. My wife is having our groceries delivered because she's afraid to leave the house. Of course, the store is charging an extra price for time and gas. I'll make copies at headquarters and start distributing them to everyone."

Jesse shook his hand. "Thanks for coming. I'll walk you to the door."

While Jesse left the kitchen, Lydia made herself some tea and stood at the window overlooking the backyard. Mitch and Brutus were basking in the sun. With Mitch in her bedroom last night, she'd actually slept nine hours, which surprised her because in strange places she didn't normally sleep well. But the mental and physical exhaustion took over the minute she laid her head on the pillow.

Jesse entered the kitchen and poured another cup of coffee. "With the dogs out back, I think we're secure since Officer Williams is sitting in the living room with a good view of the front yard."

Lydia turned from the window. "When are we going to the hospital?"

"Bree was going to figure out a good time and text me."

"She got it cleared for us to bring Mitch." Lydia returned to the table, sat and drank some of her tea.

"I have another sketch I'd like to show you." He unfolded a photocopied sheet and passed it to Lydia. "Have you seen this man?"

Lydia examined a man with short sandy hair and gray eyes, plain features with nothing that stood out, and yet there was something that nagged her. She couldn't pinpoint what.

"Have you seen him?" Jesse stood behind her, looking over her shoulder.

The hairs on her nape tingled. "Maybe. I'm usually good with faces, but not necessarily where I might have seen that person."

"So you can't say if he was in the bistro or not."

"No, just that he seems familiar. Why do you have this sketch? Who gave this description?"

"A man who worked in the appliance store across the street from the bistro. This guy was in the store when the bomb went off and seemed interested in what was going on. He hung around for a while until everyone was told to evacuate the street. Most people fled when the bomb went off."

"But there are always some who hang around to see what's going on." Lydia studied the sketch again. "You know the gawkers who stand around watching a fire, a wreck or something like that."

"When I was checking that side of the street before we got the go-ahead to search for survivors, all the buildings were supposed to be empty. I saw someone going out the back door at the appliance store. The owner said he and his employees left and thought that the store was vacant."

"You think it could have been this guy?"

"When I checked out back, a black Chevy peeled away from the parking lot. We haven't been able to find it yet. "

"If that is the case, this guy doesn't look like the orderly. He's older than the orderly. Could there be more than one person?" The thought of two or more maniacs out there knotted her stomach, her body tensing.

Jesse clasped her shoulders. "I won't rest until we get this guy or guys." His strong hands kneaded her tight muscles as he spoke. "The man might have hired someone to go to the hospital, so it still might be just one person. This last bomb site has garnered more leads than the other two put together. Those bombs went off when not many people were there, not like the bistro."

"Trial runs?" Slowly the tension melted under his expert manipulations.

"Could be that, or he's getting bolder or refining his MO." He squeezed her shoulders, then took the chair kitty-corner from her. "How's Kate taking this? She stayed in your room most of the evening."

"My sister is scared, but she's also mad that she has to be guarded. She wants to be safe but free."

"Kate probably has nothing to worry about, but I prefer being extra cautious rather than regretting a decision after the fact."

"I know one thing. Come Monday morning, she'll be eager to go to school. Most Mondays I have to drag her out of bed to get her up."

He chuckled. "I seem to remember you used to have trouble getting up, too. There were several Mondays you were late for school."

His teasing look flushed her cheeks with warmth. "I'm still that way. I've been known to be late Monday for work, and I can't always blame it on Kate."

"Blame what on me?" her sister asked from the doorway.

Lydia glanced at her. "Being late for work on Monday."

Kate harrumphed and shuffled toward the coffeepot. "Where are your mugs?"

"In the cabinet right above."

"Thanks," her sister mumbled, then retrieved one and poured coffee into it. "That was the last of it. I can make more."

"Unless you want more. I'm fine." Jesse took a long drink of his.

Kate made her way to the table and plopped down.

Her long brown hair was a tangled mess, and she finger combed it. "I can't believe I slept so late."

"So you slept all right?" Lydia finished her tea.

"Better than I thought I would." Kate smiled at Jesse. "Thanks for having us and letting Mitch stay in our bedroom."

Lydia pressed her lips together before she laughed out loud. When Kate wanted something, she could turn on the charm, and in this case she wanted to see Connor. Lydia relaxed back and waited to see what her sister would say.

"Since we can't go anywhere, I was wondering…" she lowered her gaze for a few seconds then reestablished visual contact with a contrite expression on her face "…if I could have a friend over here. Two days staying inside with such beautiful weather is a long time without at least seeing someone. Please." Kate batted her eyelids.

Lydia dug her teeth into her lower lip and fought to keep a straight face. Jesse slid a glance toward her. "You're in charge of the protection detail, not me."

The look he sent her made it clear she would hear about it later. Then he switched his attention to Kate. "It's important that people don't know where Lydia is. It makes protecting her easier."

"Oh, that's all right. I let it slip when I was talking to Connor, so he already knows."

"You did?" His jaw twitched. "Didn't I say not to tell anyone?"

"Yes, but he's my boyfriend. We see each other every weekend."

"Video-chatting is the next best thing. Feel free to do that with him, but no visitors here."

"But I told him we'd get to see each other this weekend. That's not fair." Kate swiveled her attention between Jesse and Lydia and started to say something else when Jesse's cell phone blared the moose call.

He rose and went into the other room to answer.

"You need to convince him Connor would be all right to come visit. He isn't gonna say anything. He loves me."

"No. I told you his word was final."

Kate bolted to her feet, glared at Lydia and rushed from the room, nearly colliding with Jesse returning to the kitchen.

"I figure she isn't too happy with my answer." Jesse pocketed his cell.

"Join the list. I'm right at the top. At least once a week, I get 'you're not my mom,' which means I have no right to set boundaries."

"I noticed you deferred to me to tell her she couldn't."

"I tried, but it didn't sit well with her, so I told her this was your house and you had final say."

"Chicken."

Laughing, Lydia held up her hands, palms outward. "Yep. I'm tired of fighting with her."

"That was Bree. Jake can see us. He'll be in his room the rest of the morning."

"Good. Until he sees Mitch, he won't know how well his dog is adapting to three legs. I'll go get ready and meet you in the foyer in ten minutes." Lydia rose.

Jesse took several steps toward her, shrinking the space between them. "She'll come around. You used to get mad at your dad when you were stuck at home babysitting Kate."

"But at least you got to come over and help."

"This will pass. She'll appreciate you one day. It took me a while to realize how much my last foster parents did for me."

"Do you see them much?"

"After church on Sunday, I usually eat with them, but I won't this weekend."

"Surely someone else can guard us while you get some downtime."

"It wouldn't help. I'd worry the whole time."

"You'd worry about me?"

He framed her face. "Yes. My job is to protect you, and I wouldn't relax much wondering if you were all right or not."

Did that mean he had forgiven her about Aaron? That they could be friends at least? She didn't ask because she didn't want him to tell her he would feel that way about anyone he was assigned to protect. For a while she wanted to think she was special to him. It made this whole situation bearable.

"Wait until I get Mitch out of the back." Jesse climbed from his SUV at the hospital, and once he had the K-9 harnessed, he came around to Lydia's passenger door and opened it.

He held out his hand to help her down, and she fit hers in his. He wished he could say her touch meant nothing to him, but he couldn't. Having Lydia in his home had affected him more than he thought it would. For years, he'd fooled himself into thinking he was over Lydia. But this morning, seeing her in his kitchen, he realized he wasn't. He cared, and he didn't want to. Every close tie he'd allowed himself to have had ended badly. He wasn't going through that again.

"I hope this helps Jake recover faster." Lydia's soft voice pulled him from his dilemma.

Its sound flowed through him, sparking a need he'd kept buried for years and making a mockery of his earlier declaration to keep his distance. When she was safe, he would stay away from her, but right now he was responsible for protecting her and hoped she could remember enough to catch this bomber before he struck again. Then he could get back to the way things were before.

"I know if I were in his shoes, I'd want to see Brutus. Jake and Mitch have been partners for years."

"How long have you and Brutus worked together?"

"Six." Jesse opened the hospital door and waited for Lydia to go inside first.

"No wonder you two are such a good team. Like an old married couple."

"Yeah, I'm married to my job."

Lydia pushed the elevator button. "Is that why you don't have a wife?"

The doors swished open, and Jesse entered the elevator after Lydia, relieved another couple got on, too. It gave him time to try and figure out what to reply. When they exited on Jake's floor, he started down the corridor, hoping Lydia would forget the question.

But as she walked beside him, she slanted a look at him. "You have so much to offer a woman."

"It's not like I'm a hermit, but between being a K-9 officer and taking part in search and rescues, my time has been limited." He stopped outside Jake's room and faced her. "Why haven't you remarried? You and Aaron have been divorced for years."

"Two reasons, my schooling and then work took so much of my time, and I'm gun-shy."

"Sounds like we have that in common."

"All-consuming work or being gun-shy?"

"Both." Jesse knocked on the door, then pushed it open.

Jake's grandfather shook hands with Jesse who introduced Lydia to him.

"I'm going to the cafeteria to get something to eat." Mr. Nichols bent to pet Mitch, and then he left.

His head wrapped in a white bandage, Jake sat partway up in his bed, his leg in a cast and suspended in the air. "This has been difficult for him. He's hardly left this room since the accident. I've told him I'm getting better and to go to my home and get a good night's rest, but my grandfather can be stubborn." Jake's gaze fell on Mitch. "Come, boy."

The German shepherd hobbled toward Jake and managed to lean his front legs on the bed while supporting himself with his hind one. Jake leaned forward and rubbed his K-9, tears shining in his eyes. He buried his face against Mitch. "Thanks for bringing him here." Jake's thickened voice underscored the emotional tie he had with his partner.

Jesse could identify with that. What would he do if something happened to Brutus? Until this moment he'd refused to think about that.

Lydia approached the other side of the bed. "I did what I could. I'd hoped I could save his leg, but it wasn't possible."

Jake swung his attention to her. "I knew he was in good hands with you. You remind me of your dad. He'd do anything to save an animal and give it the best life possible. Mitch can't be a police K-9 dog, but he can do other things with his training."

Lydia glanced at Mitch "He's amazed me how fast he's adapted to having three legs."

"Yeah, he's always been a quick learner and has a streak of determination a mile wide." Jake turned to Jesse. "He reminds me of your Brutus. Everything okay with them together?"

"Brutus has a playmate. You should see them in my backyard."

"And Mitch is guarding me and Kate at night in our bedroom."

"He's a good guard dog and tracker. But he's also cross-trained to detect drugs. His career isn't over. It'll just be different." Jake sank back against his pillows but kept his hand on Mitch's paw. "Tell me what's going on with the investigation. My grandfather won't tell me anything."

Jesse went through what they knew, but toward the end, Jake's eyelids slid closed. "Jake?" He looked at all the machines his friend was hooked up to, and everything seemed all right.

"We wore him out." Lydia rounded the end of the bed. "I know how exhausted you can get from even carrying on a conversation when you've been injured."

"We accomplished what we wanted to do. I think he'll rest better after seeing Mitch. Let's go."

Seeing Jake with Mitch touched a deep chord in Jesse. He loaded the German shepherd into the back of his SUV and slipped behind the steering wheel, but he didn't start the car. Remembering the tears in Jake's eyes when he greeted Mitch made Jesse confront a concern that he'd refused to acknowledge until he'd seen Jake.

Finally Jesse started the SUV and grasped the steering wheel. What was he going to do if he lost Brutus? His Rottweiler was eight, and his years as a K-9 partner were limited. He would have to break in a new dog, but worse he would have to deal with the loss of Brutus eventually.

"What's wrong?" Lydia's question penetrated the fear he'd been holding at bay for years—having to handle yet another loss. He should be used to it by now—after his family and Lydia, but...

"Jesse?"

He blinked and glanced toward her.

"What happened? You're pale."

"Seeing Jake and Mitch was hard. That could be me and Brutus at any time. In fact, we've had a few narrow escapes in the years we've worked together. I should be used to death, to goodbyes."

"I don't think anyone totally is immune to them. I think instead we ignore the emotions generated as if they don't exist, but one day they'll come to the surface. When my baby died, I refused to talk about her death, after all I never got to hold her. I tried to convince myself she didn't really exist. Then one day I was holding a friend's two-month-old girl and everything crashed down on me. That's when I really began to mourn her."

He squeezed his hands around the steering wheel and gritted his teeth. "I don't think I ever mourned my parents' deaths."

"You went to a service for them, didn't you?"

"Yes. My foster mother at that time took me, and people from my dad's work paid tribute to him. The caskets were closed. For the longest time I didn't understand why, but then I became involved in search and rescue and found my first body in the wilderness left to the elements and animals. Then I realized why no one would let me see them."

"You never told me how they died."

"They were park rangers who got caught in a sudden blizzard early in the season. Everything changed after that. Fear became part of my life until I just shut it all down."

Lydia laid her hand on his arm. "I'm so sorry."

Her touch pulled him away from the past, and he shook his head. "Everyone suffers losses. Life goes on." He never talked about his parents, and he realized the reason why. It opened up too many memories. He pried his hand from the steering wheel and flexed his fingers, then put his SUV in Reverse. "We need to get home. Chance is coming to take my place while I track down some leads. The sooner we find this man, the quicker we can get back to our normal lives." And then he could put Lydia in proper perspective.

When they arrived at his house Chance's state trooper car was out front. "I'm glad we've gotten some assistance from the state police. The sketches from this morning are being circulated and will be on the news. Maybe someone will recognize the person in either of the drawings."

Lydia slid from his SUV in his garage. Before she opened the door to the house, she turned toward him. "I'm a good listener if you ever want to talk about your parents. I joined a support group after my baby died, and it really helped."

"They died twenty-five years ago. I'm fine."

"Are you? You were left alone at a vulnerable age."

Jesse reached around her and shoved his door open. "I have work to do."

As he retrieved Brutus from the backyard, the hurt that flashed into Lydia's eyes niggled his conscience and made him regret his abrupt end to their conversation. She was getting to him again, and he needed to keep his focus on finding the bomber and keeping her alive. Then he could move on with no regrets.

"I thought Officer Williams would be guarding me at work today," Lydia said as she climbed into Jesse's SUV on Monday.

Jesse pulled out of the garage and headed toward the animal hospital. "He will be there. He's meeting us. I'll take you to and from work. Officer Williams will be out in the reception area while Officer Collins will drop Kate at school, then come and relieve me as your guard. Then I'll relieve her later, so she can pick up Kate from school. She'll take her to my house and stay with her until you leave work with me."

"You've changed things around."

"With work and school the schedule needed to be adjusted. Chance has agreed to be one of the guards at night. During the day I'll be helping Thomas run down leads, but if for any reason you need to talk to me, call me."

She tried to relax, but tension knotted her neck and shoulder muscles. She wanted—needed—to get back to work. Sitting around resting was driving her crazy because she couldn't remember anything to help the police. Maybe getting back to work would help her.

"I think I'm trying too hard to remember and nothing is coming."

"Probably. Have you ever forgotten a name or some tidbit of info, and as long as you try to concentrate on the answer, nothing comes to mind, but hours or even days later you remember?"

"Sure, but we don't have days."

"I want you to know we're making some progress. There are several names connected to both the hardware store and church."

Lydia angled toward Jesse, taking in his strong profile, remembering the times she'd freely touched his face, kissed him. No, she had to forget those times. Too much had happened since then. Staring out the windshield, she brought her thoughts back to their conversation. "How about the bistro?"

"That's a bit harder, but there is a waitress who's been on vacation and we're trying to get in touch with her. She may be able to help us with some of the names on the list at the other two bomb sites. Did someone frequent all three or even two of the places?"

"How about me? I go—went to the bistro at least once a week. I know some names, but I mostly remember faces. If you have a picture with a name, I could take a look."

"I'll have that for you tonight." Jesse pulled into the parking lot next to the animal hospital.

As he and Brutus escorted her into the building, Jesse scanned his surroundings, his gaze lingering on where the bistro used to be. His mouth firmed into a fierce look. Lydia followed the direction he stared and shivered. Every time she came to work, she would remember what happened that day the bomb went off. She would never forget it.

"I wish this place wasn't on the same street," she said as Jesse reached around her and opened the door.

Inside, some of the stress of seeing the bomb site faded as she saw familiar faces and surroundings. She greeted the staff as she made her way to her office with Jesse and Brutus. She put her purse in the drawer of her desk while Brutus and Jesse walked around the room.

"Everything all right?" she asked, slipping into the white coat she wore over her clothes.

After he completed his inspection, Jesse looked at her. "It seems to be. I wish I could leave Brutus with you, but the people I'm interviewing are people who have ties to the hardware store and the church. If one of them worked with the bombing materials, the scent could be on him, and Brutus will be able to alert me."

The idea that he would offer to do that touched her. "It wouldn't work anyway. Brutus is well trained, but I can't take him into an exam room when I have a patient. Some animals aren't well trained like he is, and there could be a problem." She could imagine the chaos it would cause with certain pets, especially cats and high-strung dogs.

"We'll at least walk through the whole building each morning and when I come back in the afternoon. I know Williams will be out in reception so that should be enough, but you can't be too cautious."

"We're going to be fine with two officers and an alert staff. I want you out there tracking down this man."

Jesse stopped in front of her. "I wish we had enough dogs trained to search for bombs. I've heard some businesses are shutting down or only letting people in they know. The thing about a bomb is it doesn't have to be left in a building to do damage. It can be placed anywhere nearby."

"All we can do then is pray the person is found quickly, and put our safety in the Lord's hands. And be as vigilant as we can." Even more lately she'd come to realize she couldn't control the actions of others and what happened around her. But she couldn't stay in her house and never leave it. The bomber found her at her home. God was the only one who could protect her ultimately.

"If anyone finds something left unattended, we're asking them to report it. That has kept our officers even busier because we're getting a ton of calls and each one has to be checked out."

"While the bomber is sitting back enjoying the fear he's caused in the city." Lydia balled her hands, her fingernails digging into her palms. "I've got to remember."

Jesse clasped her upper arms. "Listen to me. This isn't all on your shoulders. We are going to find this guy."

She nodded, trying not to put pressure on herself. It wasn't easy, though. The urge to press herself against Jesse and wrap her arms around him flooded her. He made her feel safe as though the Lord had sent him to guard over her.

"Good. Now give me a tour of the hospital."

Jesse followed her into the hallway, Lydia very aware of him behind her. She walked him through the examination rooms and Matt's office. They ended up in the break room where she fixed him a coffee to go.

JoAnn appeared in the doorway. "We have an emergency. Are you ready to see an American Eskimo dog?"

"What kind of emergency?"

"He's alive but hardly responding. His master just carried him inside. And Officer Collins is here."

"Put the owner and dog in exam room one, and show Officer Collins back here."

"I already did." JoAnn smiled.

"I'm leaving. See you this afternoon." Jesse smiled at her and headed for the hallway as the female police officer came into the break room.

Lydia snatched an extra white coat from a hanger and gave it to Mary. "Put this on over your uniform. I'm going to introduce you as an intern, here observing. I don't want to frighten people any more than they already are with what's been happening."

Mary slipped into the white coat that came to her knees and hid her gun belt, then removed her hat.

"I have an emergency patient." Lydia left the break room at a brisk pace with the police officer right behind her.

Once she stepped into the exam room one, she went into professional mode, her gaze falling on a white furry dog on the table, lying listlessly. Then his legs twitched, and he tried to get up.

JoAnn moved in to calm the animal while Lydia turned to the owner, an older gentleman, with gray hair and beard, his shoulders slumped forward. "What happened?"

"I had a box of candy on the counter, and he somehow knocked it onto the floor and ate some chocolate." The man's eyes misted. "I thought it was out of reach."

"How much chocolate?"

"A lot. Most of the box." The man closed his eyes and rubbed his hand across his forehead. "Fifteen, twenty pieces maybe. He started vomiting and having seizures. He could barely walk. I grabbed him and put him in the car, then came here. You were the nearest vet. Can you help him?"

This wasn't the first time she'd seen a dog poisoned by chocolate, which could be lethal to them. "Was it white, milk or dark chocolate?" She positioned herself on the other side of the table from JoAnn and listened to the animal's rapid heartbeat.

"I'm not sure. No white. A mix of milk and dark. I'm never gonna have any chocolate in my house again. Please help Calvin."

"We will. You'll need to leave him here at least overnight. Okay?"

"Anything."

"I'll try to counteract the theobromine which is making him sick, and give him some medication to control his heart rate and seizures. My assistant will show you to the front to fill out the paperwork. Is this the first time you've come here?"

"Yes."

"We'll need your contact information, and I'll keep you updated." She walked the older gentleman, who limped, to the door. "JoAnn, we're moving Calvin to the treatment room."

The second the owner left, Lydia released a long breath. As she picked up the dog to move him, he began another seizure as Mary hurried around to open the door.

"Calvin, I'm going to make you better," Lydia said in her soothing voice, praying she could save him.

* * *

Jesse had worked his way through two-thirds of the people—many of whom had stopped at the hardware store and attended his church. There had been a few visitors that Pastor Paul couldn't recognize. Nothing jumped out in the interviews and Brutus hadn't alerted him to the scent of C-4 or any kind of bombing material. But there had been a few on the list of twenty who weren't home. He had to ask their whereabouts the days of the explosions, but he'd run out of time. He had six more to question tomorrow. There were times he felt like he was chasing his tail.

Tired and disappointed, he pulled into the parking lot to the animal hospital. The thought of seeing Lydia picked up his spirits as he and Brutus made their way inside. He paused in the doorway and surveyed the area. Two women were waiting, one with a poodle and another with a cat in a carrier. He headed toward Williams, a bored expression on his face. When he saw Jesse, he straightened.

"I gather nothing exciting happened here today." Jesse could remember his own assignments that consisted of standing around, watching and waiting for something to happen.

"It's been slow. Dr. McKenzie told me there have been a few cancellations for routine yearly checkups. I can't blame people for that."

"Then it's been a successful day if nothing happened. Are these two ladies the last for the day?"

"I think another one is coming and that should be it unless there's an emergency like this morning."

"I heard about that. What was it?"

"At lunch I found out it was an overdose of chocolate."

"That'll do it to some dogs. Did he make it?"

Williams nodded. "Dr. McKenzie has two more patients and after that she wants to check Calvin, the dog who ate too much chocolate. Then she'll be ready to leave. I think the day has been long for her."

Jesse approached the receptionist. "Where is Dr. McKenzie?"

"Exam room two."

He walked down the hall, rapped on the door and opened it. Officer Collins saw him and said goodbye to Lydia and then left to pick up Kate at school. He stood in the corridor, watching Lydia finish up with a beagle and then escort the young lady with her dog on a leash out into the hallway.

"The medicine should take care of her allergies. If you can, and I know it can be hard with Lady, keep her inside for a while to give the pills a chance to work."

The woman smiled. "Thank you. She was scratching so much she was bleeding. I'm glad you're all right, Dr. McKenzie." The lady glanced at Jesse.

"Officer Hunt is a friend from high school," she said as she strolled a few feet down the hall.

When Lydia came back toward Jesse, Brutus took a whiff of the air and moved closer to her. The K-9 sniffed her white coat, then sat in front of her and gave one bark.

Jesse stiffened. "He smells a component of a bomb on you."

NINE

Lydia heard the words Jesse said, but for a moment their meaning didn't register. A bomb ingredient? What? How?

"Take off your coat and let me see if it's on your slacks or shirt. Something on you has triggered Brutus." While Lydia took it off, Jesse said to Brutus, "Good boy," then gave him a treat.

As Jesse went into the storage room at the end of the hall, he said, "I'm hiding the coat, then I'm going to see if he does the same thing."

When he returned, Lydia followed him and Brutus. Her heartbeat galloped as though she'd run a mile at full speed. How did she get the scent on her? She held her breath while Brutus checked the area and sat, then barked at a cardboard box.

Jesse retrieved the coat from behind the carton. "Do you have a paper bag? I'm going to take this to the lab and see if they can tell what Brutus is smelling."

"Yes, there are some in the break room." Lydia's legs shook as she made her way there.

Jesse and Brutus were right behind her. "I'm going to assume it's connected to this case until the lab tells me otherwise." He dropped the coat into the sack. "So the question now is how did this happen?"

She shook her head. "It could be anything. I handled animals all day."

"I want to evacuate the building while I walk through with Brutus and see if he can detect it anywhere else. I'll have Officer Williams guard you outside in my SUV." Jesse started for the front of the hospital. "Who's all here?"

"I'll let Matt and his assistant know. They're in exam room three. JoAnn is getting my last patient."

As Jesse disappeared through the door into the reception area, Lydia swiped her hand across her sweaty forehead and hurried to let her partner know what was going on. In the doorway, she called him out into the hall.

Matt frowned. "What's wrong?"

"Brutus detected a bomb ingredient on my coat. Jesse is evacuating everyone. I think more as a precaution."

Matt settled his hand on her shoulder. "I'll let Chris and Mrs. Marlowe know. We'll be right out."

"I'm so sorry, Matt. I shouldn't have come back to work. I put everyone in danger."

"Let's not jump to conclusions. We don't know what's going on." He squeezed her shoulder and turned to go back into the exam room.

Lydia rushed down the corridor, her heart beating as fast as her steps. In the reception area, Officer Williams waited for her. "Where's Jesse?"

"Outside with the staff and people in the building. He wanted to make sure no one else triggered a response from Brutus. Then he's going to go through the building. He's called Detective Caldwell." He escorted her to the parking lot at the side of the building.

Brutus sat in front of JoAnn, and Jesse instructed her to remove her coat.

Lydia watched the scene as though she were viewing a movie, not really part of what was happening, just an observer. If only that were the case.

Five minutes later after sending everyone but JoAnn and Lydia home, Jesse reentered the building. The bomb squad as well as Thomas were on the way. But he'd questioned Williams, and he reassured Jesse that he didn't see anything unusual. And yet Brutus found a suspicious scent on both Lydia's and JoAnn's coats that wasn't there when he left in the morning.

He started in the reception area with Brutus, who stopped, sat and barked in front of one of the chairs. But there was nothing around it that could be a bomb. Jesse put a marker on the chair and continued the walk through. Exam room one was another place that Brutus indicated the scent. Jesse searched the whole place, but nothing appeared to be a bomb.

When he checked a room next door, again Brutus smelled the steel table and area around it and sat immediately. An animal had left its scent on it?

When he reached the area where the sick or recovering dogs were kept, once again Brutus gave the sign he'd sniffed an ingredient in a bomb. An American Eskimo was still hooked up to an IV.

His phone rang, and he answered, "Thomas, I've almost completed my search of the building. Brutus has found several places, but there isn't a bomb. Is the bomb squad here?"

"Yes, they're moving the people and animals away from the veterinary hospital and evacuating the surrounding stores. I'll send in the commander. You two will need to decide what to do. I'm having Officer Williams take Lydia home."

"No. I need her to walk me through the people who were in these rooms. This could be the break we've been looking for. When it's safe in here, I need her to come back in."

Jesse wanted her as far away from the building as possible, but she and her assistant had more than likely interacted with the Laughing Bomber.

"So you think the bomber was at the animal hospital today?"

"Yes. I'll be outside after I finish my search." Jesse disconnected, wishing there were more dogs like Brutus in the city. Had this become some kind of game to the man behind the bombings?

Lydia chewed on her fingernail as she paced in a circle near Officer Williams, five hundred yards away from the animal hospital. What if a bomb went off while Jesse and Brutus were inside searching for it? *Lord, please keep them safe.*

She stopped when another man went into the building. "Who's that, Officer Williams?"

"The commander of the bomb squad."

"What's that mean?"

"Probably the sergeant found more evidence or a bomb."

Her chest constricted as if someone were trying to squeeze the breath from her lungs. She gasped for air. "Then they should be getting out of there." She began her pacing again, needing to move, to do something other than stare at the building. She felt so helpless.

No, I'm not. I have the Lord. He can give me peace. It had taken her a while after her daughter's death and Aaron's adultery to understand that. She began to pray. All she wanted was to see Jesse emerge from the animal hospital unharmed.

Ten *long* minutes later, Jesse and the commander came outside and made their way to Thomas. She started for them.

Officer Williams blocked her. "My orders are for you to remain here." He cocked a smile. "You don't want to get me in trouble, do you, Dr. McKenzie?"

"Please call me Lydia since we're going to be hanging out together for a while. What's your first name?"

"Don."

"No, Don, I don't. At least they are outside the building if it goes up." She intended to have a few words with Jesse when she spoke to him. This waiting was tying her up into knots.

Finally Jesse headed across the street toward her while the whole bomb squad went into the building. Did that mean they found a bomb and they were going to try to dismantle it?

She went around Don and took several steps toward Jesse, the grim expression on his face solidifying her stomach into a huge lump. "What's wrong? Is there a bomb inside?"

He shook his head. "But there were more traces of one of the ingredients that triggered Brutus with you and JoAnn. The bomb squad is going through the building, then I need you to go back in with me. I think the bomber was at your hospital today."

"But he didn't leave anything?"

"An American Eskimo dog."

JoAnn, who stood not far away, approached. "That would be Mr. Jacobs."

"The dog, Calvin, ingested chocolate. I remember his owner. You didn't pass him in the reception room?" Lydia tried to grasp the fact she'd possibly stood in the same room with the Laughing Bomber, not once but twice.

"I went out the back door to check the rear of the building." Jesse waved Officer Williams to join them. "The first patient this morning was an American Eskimo, a white dog. Do you remember the man who came with Calvin?"

"He was carrying the dog," Lydia said.

"So if Mr. Jacobs had the smell on him, he transferred it to the dog and that's how you and JoAnn got it on you. Did you move the animal to the room next door?"

"Yes, that's where I washed out his stomach and gave him activated charcoal. We started an IV, too. When he was stabilized, Calvin was transferred to the area where we keep an eye on the recovering animals. I'd planned to call Mr. Jacobs to let him know his dog was getting better, but we wanted to keep him at least overnight."

"But you haven't yet?" Jesse asked.

Lydia shook her head. "I was going to check on Calvin one more time before I made the call."

"We need his owner's address, phone number and a description. Also, I want you to make that call and tell Mr. Jacobs he can come pick up his dog."

"He was about seventy years old and walked with a

limp and had slumped shoulders. He had gray hair and a pasty white complexion. I thought he was sickly. I don't remember the color of his eyes. JoAnn, do you?"

Her assistant thought for a moment. "Blue or gray—not dark eyes. But he'll be on our security tape."

Like the color of eyes I keep seeing in my thoughts. "Yes, we had that installed last week as one of the security measures. It's monitored by an outside source, so even if something happened to the building, there would be a record."

Jesse smiled for the first time since he arrived. "Good thinking. This is all promising."

"So you think this old man is the Laughing Bomber?" Lydia couldn't picture the frail man as a maniacal murderer.

"It's possible or he's working with materials that make up a bomb. That's what Brutus is trained to sniff out. We don't know yet if it's the ingredients in C-4. Brutus found four places in the building. A chair in the reception area, the exam room and the one next door as well as the place where you monitor the animals. Did he seem familiar to you, Lydia?"

Again she tried to run through the faces she remembered at the bistro while she was there. Again nothing but Melinda's image popped into her mind…a vision of the waitress, Eve, serving a young couple materialized. "I remember a few others, but they aren't Mr. Jacobs." She'd been looking at the photos over the weekend that Jesse had left of the victims, so was that a true memory or wishful thinking? "The waitress put two plates down at the table next to me. A young couple sat there."

"You can show me their photos when we get home. The more you remember the people who are in the photo array, the more I think you'll remember the rest of what you saw."

When we get home. If she hadn't made a bad mistake with Aaron all those years ago, she could have married Jesse.

"No one wants it more than me. This man is holding the city hostage."

Jesse glanced toward the animal hospital. "Tyler is waving at us. We can go inside. JoAnn, I want you to go, too."

"You betcha. The very idea he was in our building standing only a foot away from me gives me the willies." Without waiting, JoAnn marched across the street.

"The Laughing Bomber better watch out. JoAnn is fierce when she's on a mission." Lydia walked beside Jesse. "But she's right. The 'willies' are a good description of how I feel."

"I'm not going to let anything happen to you." A steel resolve laced each of Jesse's words. "You can't go to work until we find this guy. He hasn't given up trying to get to you."

"I agree. While I was waiting for you to come outside, I told Matt I wouldn't be back tomorrow. He's thinking of closing down the animal hospital and sending everyone on vacation for the next week at least."

"He wouldn't be the first. I've heard of a couple of other places closing, too."

"He thinks he can make house calls if one of our clients has an emergency."

Jesse introduced the bomb squad commander to her, and she shook his hand. "I'm glad you didn't find a bomb. That it was a false alarm."

"We've been kept busy this past week with false alarms, but I'd rather people be cautious and call than the alternative. I've collected the evidence to see if we can narrow down the ingredient Brutus smelled. I'll put a rush on it. We should hear back soon."

Lydia and JoAnn entered the building with Jesse with Brutus while Thomas kept the others out until they retraced their steps. JoAnn stopped at the reception desk and found the contact information for Mr. Jacobs and gave it to Jesse.

Then Lydia proceeded through what she and JoAnn did with the American Eskimo. The only places Calvin went were where Brutus indicated.

"JoAnn, you've been a big help. You can let the others come in." Jesse waited until she disappeared down the hallway. "Lydia, let's go into your office and give Mr. Jacobs a call about Calvin."

She sat at her desk and picked up the phone, her hand trembling as she punched in the numbers the old man had left. She let it ring ten times before she hung up. "No answer."

"I'm taking you home and then Thomas and I are going to the address he gave JoAnn. I'll have Officer Williams stay until I get back."

"Just the two of you are going? He could be the bomber."

"Reinforcements will be hiding, waiting for a signal from us if we think it's him or he makes a run for it."

"I can't imagine Mr. Jacobs running. And he looks nothing like the drawing of the man in the appliance store or the fake orderly who was in my room."

"I know. This case has more questions than answers."

"Do you want me to continue trying to call him?"

"No. Let me see what we discover first. Are you ready to leave?"

"In a minute. I have a couple of animals to check on."

"I'll come with you."

Lydia began listing in her mind all the instructions she would have to give to Matt about the animals left until their owners were able to pick them up. "There are a couple of dogs and one cat that needs to stay, but Matt should be okay if the place is locked down."

"Yes. The security system is good, or I would never have let you come to work at all."

The intensity in his look and voice made her feel protected but also something more. If she didn't know better she would think that Jesse cared about her. Of course, he cared if she were safe. That was the kind of person he was. Expecting more was setting herself up to be hurt—like she'd hurt him.

Jesse pulled up in front of a small white house, well kept, with a fenced backyard. The blackout shades were down on every window they could see. The hairs on his nape tingled. It didn't feel right. He called Thomas, who was behind him in his car. "It doesn't look like anyone is home."

"Let's park up the street. Maybe we should check with a couple of neighbors to find out about Mr. Jacobs. He isn't the man who owns this house, and there isn't a driver's license for the guy."

"He won't be the first person to drive without a license. And the house is listed as a rental."

"But I haven't gotten in touch with the owner to see

who is occupying it right now. I'll take the neighbor on the right. You visit the one on the left."

Jesse parked and unloaded Brutus from the rear, then approached the house on the left. He rang the doorbell and waited. Turning, he noticed a car in the driveway so this time he knocked. Still no answer. He decided to go across the street and see if that person was home.

An older woman, probably in her late sixties, opened her door but left the half glass/half screen shut. "Is something wrong, Officer?"

"Do you know your neighbor directly across the street?"

"No one has been there for a while or at least no one I've seen. I keep an eye on the street since I'm home all the time. I thought Mr. Sims would have rented it by now, but he hasn't put up a sign."

"Who lived there last? We haven't been able to get in touch with Mr. Sims yet."

"A young man, not very friendly. I'd say hi to him, and he would ignore me."

"Did this man have a dog?"

"If he did, I never saw it." The petite woman frowned. "What's going on? Is something wrong?"

Jesse glanced at Thomas talking to a man on a porch. "Do you know a gentleman around seventy years old? Mr. Jacobs?"

She shook her head and unlocked her screen door, then stepped out on her stoop and pointed toward the man Thomas was talking to. "That's his name. But as you can see, he isn't seventy."

Jesse removed a business card. "If you see anyone at the house across the street, please give me a call."

The lady's brown eyes widened. "What's this about?"

"It has to do with a case I'm investigating."

Her mouth twisted in a thoughtful expression. "I can call. I figure you have your hands full with the Laughing Bomber. I don't leave much so I might see something." She looked at the card and slipped it in her dress pocket. "I'm Anna Dodson."

"Could you describe the man who used to live there?"

"I could hardly see his face with all the hair and beard. He was normal height, certainly not as tall as you. Thin. Probably no more than thirty but again not sure."

"Thanks." Jesse turned to leave.

"What's your dog's name?"

He looked back and grinned. "Brutus."

"He's well behaved. I used to have a dog that would never sit that long. Always getting into things."

"Good day, Ms. Dodson."

Jesse met Thomas in the yard of the house in question. "Did Mr. Jacobs tell you no one has been here for a while?"

"Yes, at least a few weeks. And while I was talking to him, the owner, Mr. Sims, called me. He didn't realize it wasn't occupied. The man living here, a Sam Alexander, paid the rent this month. I asked him if we had permission to go inside. He gave it and is actually on his way here with the key."

"While we're waiting for him, I'm going to take Brutus around the house and check out what's in the backyard. See if he picks up anything." Jesse nodded his head toward the neighbor to the right. "I know Mr.

Jacobs doesn't fit the description Lydia and JoAnn gave us, but do you think he could be involved somehow?"

"I'll be checking him out. And I'll send someone out to talk to the neighbor to the left. When I saw you walking across the street, I asked Mr. Jacobs if they worked. It's a middle-aged couple, and they both work at the hospital."

Jesse started across the yard, letting Brutus sniff around while he checked if he could see inside, but all the shades were pulled. When he tried the back door, the knob turned. He wanted to go inside, but he didn't want any legal issues. This case was too important. Jesse completed circling the house as a white Ford Escort pulled into the driveway.

Mr. Sims greeted Thomas, then Jesse, but as the owner started for the house, Thomas said, "I'd prefer you stay outside. We don't know what we'll find inside."

"But it's my place."

"As soon as we think it's safe, you're welcome to come inside, but there's a possibility this place is tied to a crime and therefore there may be evidence we don't want compromised."

Mr. Sims opened his mouth but snapped it closed before saying anything. He nodded.

Jesse took the key the owner held out for them and walked toward the porch. "Let me and Brutus go first. For some reason the fake Mr. Jacobs went to a lot of trouble to send us here."

His K-9 sniffed around the porch and especially the entrance. Jesse waited until he was through before unlocking the door. He eased it open, looking for any trip wires. Then Jesse and Brutus entered going to the right. His K-9 checked the living room for any scent of a bomb.

Thomas came to the doorway. "Okay for me to come in?"

"So far nothing. But you should stay there until I check everything." Jesse strolled into the dining room and stepped onto an area rug where a table and four chairs were.

Brutus went to the right, smelling a cabinet. He sat and barked.

"Get out," Jesse yelled.

Following his friend, Jesse ran for the door with Brutus.

Two feet from the exit, a laughing track sounded.

TEN

When the doorbell rang at Jesse's house, Lydia came from the kitchen to see Officer Williams checking the peephole, then opening the door with his hand on his gun handle.

"Yes?" Don asked the teenage boy on the porch.

"Kate invited me over."

"Wait here." As Lydia walked toward the hallway to the bedroom they shared at Jesse's house, she wanted to throttle her sister. After the day she'd had at work, this was not what she wanted to deal with.

When she turned the corner, Lydia spied Kate coming out of the room. Lydia hurried her steps and blocked her sister's path. "Where do you think you're going?"

"I saw Connor's car parked out front."

"Did you invite him over here?"

Kate lifted her chin and narrowed her eyes. "So what if I did? I need help with my Algebra II homework. Who do you think has been tutoring me?"

"This is the first I've heard that you needed a tutor. Why didn't you tell me this earlier?"

"You haven't been home but ten minutes. Connor is early." Kate started around Lydia.

But she stepped to the side, preventing her sister from going anywhere. "Is that the truth or another lie?"

"What lie?" Kate's voice rose several decibels.

"You did great last year in geometry. Math has never given you a problem before."

"How would you know? Until this year you were never around."

"You made a B in Algebra I."

Kate got in Lydia's face. "Because I had a tutor. If you hadn't stayed away, you'd have known that."

Lydia took a step back, her pulse racing at the anger pouring off her sister.

"You left me here with Dad. He didn't care what I did. So why do you? Mom left, you left and then Dad…"

The issues that had been standing between them spewed out. A lot of what Kate was feeling, Lydia had gone through herself—a bit differently but the end result was the same, the feeling of abandonment.

Kate opened and closed her hands at her sides, her glare cutting through Lydia.

"You two can work at the dining room table if Officer Williams says it is okay."

Her sister charged past Lydia while she gathered her composure. She'd never felt that she'd abandoned her little sister, but in her eyes she had. They would have to talk about this. This anger couldn't continue, especially when a mad bomber might have been at her place of work today.

She made her way toward the foyer, Kate's pleading voice drifting to her.

Don glanced at Lydia when she came into view.

"It's your call, Don. If you aren't sure, you should call Jesse and ask him."

At that moment Officer Collins entered the living room with Mitch beside her. She looked at everyone, then asked, "I think the neighbors heard the shouting." She directed her look right at Kate. "With all that's been going on, nothing can be that bad."

Kate pinched her lips together.

"Thanks for bringing Mitch in." Lydia stooped to hug the German shepherd.

Kate gave Don a huge smile and turned her back on Lydia. "Please let Connor stay. I need help with our homework. Promise."

Don withdrew his cell phone. "I'm calling the sergeant."

Kate's shoulder sagged forward.

When Don clicked off, he looked up. "He isn't answering." His forehead crinkled. "I guess since you're here you can stay at least until he comes home."

Kate grabbed Connor's hand and pulled him toward the dining room so quickly Lydia almost laughed.

She straightened and moved toward Don, lowering her voice, "I think she's afraid you'll change your mind. I'm surprised Jesse didn't answer."

"So am I. Maybe they've got a good lead with Mr. Jacobs."

Lydia hoped that was the case. Before the Laughing Bomber totally turned this town—her life—upside down.

Against the backdrop of hideous laughter, Jesse ran behind Thomas and Brutus off the porch. A blast exploded behind him. Its force flung Jesse through the air and crashing against the hard ground. Air rushed from his lungs. His ears rang. Stunned, he tried to lift his head, but the world spun around. He collapsed back onto the grass.

Brutus. Thomas.

They were ahead of him. Maybe they were all right. Jesse drew on a reserve buried deep inside him and pushed himself up, supporting his weight as he scanned the yard. Brutus lay still a few feet from him. As Jesse crawled toward his dog, he scanned the area for Thomas. He couldn't lose either one.

To the left Thomas rolled over, shock reflected in his expression. His mouth moved, but Jesse couldn't hear what he was saying. The sound of Jesse's heartbeat thundering in his ears overpowered every other noise. He pointed to his ears. Thomas nodded his head once and removed his phone from his pocket.

Jesse continued toward Brutus and stopped next to him. His hand shook as he reached out and touched him. A movement under his palm sent a wave of relief flowing through him.

"Take it easy, Brutus," Jesse said the words, but he could barely hear himself.

His Rottweiler shook his head and tried to stand but wobbled and fell down.

Seeing his dog struggling, Jesse gathered Brutus to him and held him. "We're alive because of you. We'll be okay." Jesse didn't know if his K-9 heard him or not, but Brutus could feel Jesse's support as he stroked him. He thought of Mitch and what happened. He didn't know what he would do if he lost Brutus.

Not another loss. Please, Lord.

* * *

Five minutes after Officer Williams called Jesse, Lydia tried his number, surprised again that he didn't answer her call or Don's. Did something happen?

When the doorbell rang, she was nearest the door and hurried to see who it was. She looked out the peephole and saw Chance. She started to open the door when Don's hand clasped her arm.

"Let me answer the door. You know the drill."

"It's Chance, your replacement."

"He's early." The police officer gently pushed her back and put his body between her and the opening of the door. "Is something wrong?" Don looked around the state trooper.

"I was told to come here. There's been another bombing. A house this time."

Lydia stepped around Don. "Where?"

Chance told her the address she'd given for Mr. Jacobs.

The strength flowed from her legs, and she sank back against the police officer, who clasped her arms to hold her up. "Who's injured?" *Not Jesse. Please, Lord. I can't lose him.*

"I don't know much. Thomas and Jesse got out before it exploded but were thrown from the blast."

"How about Brutus?" Lydia asked.

"Jesse called but said he couldn't hear me. He said he and Thomas were rallying, but Brutus was bleeding. He told me to come here and make sure you and Kate were okay."

Lydia pivoted and headed for her bedroom. "I'll be right back." When she brought her belongings from her house, she included her medical bag she kept for emergencies. She grabbed it and headed back to the foyer.

"Where do you think you're going?" Chance asked.

"You're going to take me to the bomb site while these two officers stay here with Kate."

"No, I'm not."

She stared at Chance. "If you don't take me, I'm going by any means. Brutus needs medical help." And she needed to see with her own eyes that Jesse and Thomas were all right.

His eyes cut through her.

She tilted up her chin. "My car is in Jesse's garage. I'll drive myself. You can't force me to stay here."

Chance started to say something.

"Please," Lydia added.

"Okay. It won't be the first time Jesse and me have argued about something. The bomb site is probably the safest place in town by now."

Kate came into the foyer. "You can't go. He's after you."

"We don't know what this man's agenda is. Why did he rig the house? I never take animals to their owners."

"I think this madman did this to taunt the police." Officer Collins leaned against the entrance into the living room next to Kate. "He knew if anyone would go into the house it would be police."

Kate gasped.

Lydia ground her teeth, thinking about how close she'd been to Mr. Jacobs or whatever his name really was. "None of this adds up, but I can't stand around talking about it. I need to get to Brutus. I'm his vet." She thought about how Jesse would feel if he lost his dog.

"Let's go." Chance turned toward the door. "Stay here with Kate."

As he escorted Lydia to his cruiser, he kept sweeping the area as though he expected the bomber to appear suddenly.

She wouldn't put anything past this maniac. Once she knew that everyone was all right, she had to remember what happened at the bistro. If she could recall a few details, then she could somehow recreate the whole time she was in the restaurant. Lives depended on her.

On the drive to the new bomb site, Chance said, "I know this is tough on you."

"Which part, not remembering what I saw or my past with Jesse?"

"Both. I've seen you two together. And I can imagine how hard it is on you to not be able to recall the bombing. But not surprising. Our minds have a way of protecting us against trauma."

"And remembering would be traumatic, not a relief?"

"Again, both." Chance turned onto a street with fire trucks and police cars, their red lights flashing.

The sight that riveted Lydia was the ambulance and two paramedics rolling a gurney with a body on it, covered by a white sheet. "Who died?" she asked in a breathless voice that quavered.

Chance parked and glanced at her. "I don't know, but Jesse called me. He's okay, Lydia."

Inhaling and exhaling deep breaths, she grasped her bag and opened the door. "Then what about Thomas?"

Chance scowled and strode next to her as they weaved their way through the crowd forming. When they neared the half-bombed house, Lydia saw Jesse by

Brutus on the ground with Thomas talking with the fire captain. They were both okay. She spied the Rottweiler trying to get up and Jesse calming him with his hand. Relief trembled through her as she hurried to them.

Jesse looked up, his eyebrows slashing downward. "How did you get here?"

Pointing to Chance, Lydia knelt next to Brutus, seeing the blood matting his fur with a shard of glass stuck in him. "And don't be mad at him. I would have come one way or another. Brutus needs my help. And I had to see that you were okay."

"You need to speak up. My ears are still ringing. I was calming him down so I could pull the piece out."

She knew about the hearing problems and still had a little tinnitus since the blast last week. Lydia dug into her bag, prepared a tranquilizer and gave Brutus the shot. "This will calm him and then I can remove the glass and tend to the wound. Did you see any other wounds?" She glanced up at Jesse.

His brow knitted, Jesse locked gazes with her. "You shouldn't be here, but I'm glad you are. He tried to get up and collapsed."

Lydia touched one of Jesse's ears. "Like you, he could be experiencing hearing loss, dizziness."

"Yeah, that's what I thought."

Jesse kept stroking Brutus while Lydia pulled the shard out and tended to the wound. "I'll need to stitch this up. We'll have to take him to the animal hospital. Everyone's picked up their pets except Calvin. I'd like to bring him home with us and keep monitoring him. It's obvious Mr. Jacobs won't."

Jesse withdrew his pad. "I didn't catch all of that."

Lydia applied a thick bandage to Brutus's injury, then wrote on Jesse's pad and signaled Chance.

The state trooper approached. "I found out who was on the gurney. The young man who rented the house. Mr. Sims identified him."

"I need to take Brutus to the hospital and check him out more thoroughly as well as stitch up his wound." She looked at Jesse's SUV with its windows blown out. "Will you take us in your car?"

"Yes." Chance stooped and slid his arms under the Rottweiler.

While he lifted him, she decided to write on Jesse's pad what she was going to do. He nodded and began to stand. He wobbled. She wrapped her arm around him and guided him toward the cruiser. Whether Jesse liked it or not, she was going to have Chance take him to the ER after he saw that Brutus would be all right and was settled back at his house.

Later that night, Lydia finally sank onto the couch and sighed. She was so tired she didn't know if she could get up to go to bed. She wouldn't until Chance returned with Jesse from the ER. He hadn't wanted to go, but they'd finally persuaded him. Lydia suspected the adrenaline that sometimes kept pain at bay had finally subsided. While she'd taken care of Brutus at the animal hospital, Chance had picked bits and pieces of debris from Jesse's back. Not anything large like his dog's, but the back of Jesse's shirt was bloodied.

Both Brutus and Calvin were curled up on the floor in the living room, much better and sound asleep. Connor left right after they returned home per Jesse's order. Now Lydia waited for Chance to either call or bring

Jesse home. She'd managed to chew one thumbnail down to the quick and was working on the other when the front door opened.

She shoved to her feet while Don came in the foyer from the back of the house. Mary Collins, at the other end of the couch, stood. Both were alert, but Don immediately relaxed, which meant Jesse was home. Lydia hurried toward the entry, needing to see he was okay.

Moving stiffly, Jesse stepped through the entrance with Chance right behind him. Even Kate appeared from the hallway leading to the bedrooms.

No one said anything for half a minute. Jesse's left side of his face was starting to bruise, probably where his face hit the ground. His left arm had a bandage around it and no doubt his back was a patchwork of tended wounds. He had on his short-sleeve black uniform shirt, untucked and bedraggled.

With a shadow in his eyes, he swung toward Lydia. "How's Brutus doing?"

"I think better than you. He's sound asleep and probably will be through the night. Which is what you need to do."

"I can stay through the night with Chance," Don said. "Then we can figure out tomorrow."

"I appreciate that, but, Don, this isn't going to change anything." Jesse waved his hand toward his bandaged arm. "I had minor cuts. No big deal."

Chance shook his head but remained quiet.

"There'll be a lot to do sifting through the house tomorrow. This may be the break we needed." Jesse looked from Don to Mary. "Thanks for staying late. You don't need to be here until nine. I'll make sure

Kate gets to school." He turned his attention to her sister. "We have a few things to discuss on the way."

Kate waited until Jesse trod into the living room before she spun on her heel and stormed down the hallway toward their bedroom. Her sister didn't think rules applied to her. Lydia was glad she could count on Jesse to stand strong.

Chance saw the two police officers out locking the front door. When he came into the living room, deep frown lines bracketed his mouth. "I believe I heard the ER doc telling you to rest for the next day or so."

Jesse sat on the floor near his K-9, stroking him. "I'll rest when we catch this guy. He set a trap for any police that came to search that house. If it hadn't been for Brutus being there, we wouldn't have had enough time to get out." He zeroed in on Lydia. "And I don't think the bomber is a seventy-year-old man with a limp. I think our bomber has been wearing disguises. With that in mind, Thomas wants you down at police headquarters tomorrow to give a description of the guy. Then we'll use the sketches we have to see if we can guess what he might look like. There's a computer program that looks for similarities."

"What if one of the sketches is really the bomber?" Lydia asked, still feeling as if she saw something she shouldn't have at the bistro.

"That's possible, and of course, each one is being taken seriously. Chance, I'm too wound up to go to sleep right now. I'll take the first watch."

His friend clamped his lips together, started for the spare bedroom but stopped. "Okay, but I'm relieving you in three hours. No arguments. You won't be worth anything if you don't get some rest."

Jesse nodded, then pushed to his feet, wincing once.

"Sure, you're fine." Lydia placed her hands on her waist. "If that's the case, why did you wince?"

He averted his gaze and headed toward the kitchen. Lydia followed. She wasn't going to bed until she knew he had. This happened because of her. If she hadn't gone to the animal hospital, the older gentleman wouldn't have come with Calvin. If only she could remember what the bomber thought she knew and help the police put him in jail.

Jesse stood at the counter, fixing a pot of coffee.

"It's obvious you aren't as wired as you think or you wouldn't need caffeine to stay up."

He threw her a scowl and plugged in the pot. "Chance is volunteering to help. He still has his day job to go to."

"And you shouldn't be doing anything tomorrow, but you are. Your stubbornness hasn't changed."

"I call it 'resolve.' Earlier today my foster mother phoned me to ask if I thought it was safe for her to go to the grocery store. I told her about one that's delivering."

"I've heard of other businesses doing that, but not everyone can."

Jesse leaned against the counter as the coffee perked behind. "Did you notice the traffic today? It's probably half of what it would be normally. The Laughing Bomber Task Force has doubled in size. We have help from the FBI on profiling this guy. ATF is also involved."

The tense set of his shoulder and the lines of exhaustion on his face prompted Lydia to bridge the distance between them and grasp his right forearm. "I'll bring you your coffee in the living room. At least sit on the couch where you'll be more comfortable and near Brutus."

He didn't move for a moment. Then he covered her hand for a few seconds before pushing away from the counter and trudging out of the kitchen.

When he left, Lydia tucked her hands under her armpits, closed her eyes and tried to picture the bistro when she arrived that day. She opened the door and collided with...who? A man. What did he look like? Was he a regular? Did she know him? A vague image of a middle-aged man wearing a hoodie. Odd? Usually she saw young people doing that. As much as she concentrated on bringing his features into focus, she couldn't.

Okay, she entered the bistro and made a beeline toward Bree. Then what? Who did she pass? Was the pharmacist from the drugstore sitting with...? The picture in her head faded and a black screen filled her thoughts. Her eyes popped open, and disappointment slumped her shoulders.

Lord, please. This needs to stop. Help me to remember.

But nothing came to mind.

The coffee was ready, so she poured a mug for Jesse and walked into the living room to find his head resting on the back couch cushion, his eyes closed. Quietly she put the coffee on the table and took the chair across from him. She still wanted to watch Brutus for another hour as the anesthetic wore off to make sure that he didn't try to scratch his stitches.

The urge to caress Jesse's bruised face overwhelmed her. A mistake she'd made all those years ago still haunted her with so many regrets. If she hadn't fallen for Aaron's charms, would she have ended up married to Jesse? Now she was in the middle of a horrific situation, in danger—but so was Jesse. Yes, it was his job, but if anything happened to him she'd feel it was her fault.

In that moment she realized she'd never stopped loving Jesse. He would always have a piece of her heart. But she didn't think he would ever forgive her. Like her father? He certainly hadn't forgiven her, and she had no way to repair that relationship.

She'd begun to think returning to Anchorage was a good thing in the end, especially for Kate, but also for her renewed friendships. She'd missed their support. She'd missed Jesse but hadn't realized it until they spent so much time together. They were different people, but the person she fell in love with all those years ago was still there.

Which meant he didn't share himself. He always had a part of himself he guarded closely, and she knew it stemmed from his parents' death and never really having a home. She'd pieced that much together but never from him.

Brutus stirred. Lydia rose and went to the Rottweiler to make sure everything was still all right. She placed her hand on his neck, and he settled down. She checked his wound, then stood. Her gaze collided with Jesse's.

"Is he okay?" A huskiness entered his voice.

"Yes. He's a trouper."

Jesse leaned forward and picked up the mug. "Thanks. I need this."

Lydia sat on the coffee table and stilled his hand from moving the cup to his mouth. "Don't. Take Chance up on his offer. You fell asleep just now."

"I was resting my eyes. I heard you come in."

"Really, Jesse. Don't play that macho act with me. I need you back to one hundred percent because we have to figure out who this guy is."

One of his dark eyebrows hiked up. "We?"

"Yes, tomorrow I want to talk about the bistro bombing until my memory is triggered."

"It doesn't work that way." He sat forward and put his mug on the coaster next to her.

His arm brushed hers and sent a jolt through her. What if he'd been inside the house when the bomb went off? He could have died. She covered his hands with hers. "Why not? I was waiting for the coffee to perk and I had another memory of what I witnessed in the bistro before the bomb went off."

He sat up straighter. "What?"

She told him about the people she remembered so far. "I want to look at those photos of the people killed in the bombing."

"I'll get them." He started to stand.

She halted his progress. "Sit. I'll go. Where are they?"

"On the desk in the kitchen."

She retrieved the pictures, and this time sat next to him on the couch. As she flipped through them, she was acutely aware of the man beside her, their shoulders touching. "I remember the pharmacist from the drugstore across the street, but he isn't here. He was with someone, but I can't remember her. Her! I didn't know that before, but I'm sure it was a woman, but I didn't get a good look at her—at least that I remember."

"Then we'll interview the pharmacist. I wonder why he didn't come forward. Some people did who had been there although they couldn't help us."

"Did a middle-aged man come forward? I can't remember much about the guy in the hoodie. I just thought it odd."

"I'll check with Thomas. If you can remember him, we'll have an artist draw a sketch of him." He shifted to face her. "See, you're recalling facts. Both of these might lead somewhere."

"How are you feeling, really?"

One corner of his mouth quirked. "I've had better days, but looking at you has definitely improved it." His voice and expression softened, his golden-brown eyes fixed on her face as though he were memorizing every line.

"Good. Because waiting for you to return from the ER made me a nervous wreck."

"Now you know what I went through when you were taken from the bomb site. I wanted to go in the ambulance, but I had a job that had to be done."

She ran her hand down his arm, then threaded her fingers through his. "I don't know how you did that job. I've been at search and rescue sites, but not that kind with those results, knowing most of the people you found would be dead."

"But there was always the hope we'd uncover a live person. That makes it all worth it to me, especially when Brutus found you."

Warmth suffused her face. His dreamy look held her riveted. Maybe when this was over with, they had a chance. She didn't realize how much she wanted that until that second.

He lifted his hand and cradled it against her cheek. "How are you doing through all this?"

"I'm getting better each day, but I want this to end now."

"We all do." His eyes smoldering, he combed his fingers through her hair and cupped her nape, then dragged her toward him. "I don't know what I would have done if you hadn't been alive," he whispered, his mouth an inch from hers.

Every part of her wanted him to kiss her. She inhaled sharply and let her breath out slowly as the moment hung between them. What was he waiting for?

ELEVEN

Jesse wanted to kiss her but hesitated. He felt the brush of her breath against his lips. He smelled the fruity scent that he'd come to associate with her. It comforted him—as if he'd come home.

He held her face and settled his mouth on hers. As she clasped his sides, he deepened the kiss, wanting to pour so much into it, but a part of him held back. The part that remembered the hurt. The part that had wanted to marry her and have a family with her. The part that had felt discarded every time he moved from one foster home to another.

He pulled back, his hands slipping from her face. When he did, she withdrew her touch and scooted away a few feet. She lowered her gaze and sat forward on the couch. A barrier fell between them, much like right before they broke up in December when they were seniors.

"We shouldn't have—" he said in a husky voice.

"Kissed? Why?"

"Because…because…" He didn't want to tell her he was beginning to fall in love with her.

"Never mind. It's not important. People say actions speak louder than words, and with you, that's the only way I know what's going on with you. That's not changed."

Anger shoved his doubts away. "Don't make me the bad guy in what happened between us. If actions speak louder than words, you made it clear how you really felt about me all those years ago." He pushed off the couch, grabbed his mug and left the living room.

If he hadn't, he might have said more than he wanted to. He didn't want her to know how close he'd come to telling her he wanted another chance to see if they could work out. Who was he kidding? Too much in their past stood in their way.

In the kitchen, he put the photos back on the top of the desk, then placed a call to Thomas. He'd been out of the loop and wanted to know if they discovered anything at the newest crime scene. He needed to keep his focus on the case to end this nightmare and get back to the way his life was before—what? Before Lydia came back to Anchorage? Before he was a teenage boy who fell in love with her?

"I'm glad you called," Thomas said the second he answered his phone. "I was debating whether to wait until the morning or chance waking you up. I knew you left the ER so I figure you're okay. Right?"

"I'm fine." Jesse sat back against the hard chair and flinched, making a mockery of his words. "They had to stitch a couple of my cuts up otherwise they cleaned them and sent me home." After checking his hearing and doing a CT scan on his head. "Did you go get checked out?"

"The paramedics did on-site. I was ahead of you."

"And they didn't tell you to go to your doctor."

A long pause, and then Thomas chuckled. "Okay, they did mention that, and I will when we have this guy behind bars."

"Lydia remembered a couple of things today that happened before the bomb went off." Jesse relayed what she'd told him. "I want to interview the pharmacist tomorrow. Okay?"

"Fine, but I want you to encourage Lydia to keep remembering. There's a reason the bomber has come after her and the waitress. And after today, he might be going for law enforcement. There was a message written on the only wall that withstood the blast today, 'Back off or you'll regret it.'"

"So you think it was directed at us?"

"Yes. We're checking around at other vets about an American Eskimo named Calvin since the dog seems to respond to that name. Nothing so far."

"Have you tried the pound?"

"That's next as well as putting out a picture of Calvin and asking anyone if they have seen this dog. The bomber will make a mistake. He's getting bolder and reckless. But we've got to stop him before someone else dies."

"I'll interview the pharmacist and then take Calvin by the pound. Maybe seeing him will help someone recognize him. I'll be in touch after I do that tomorrow." When Jesse hung up, he turned toward the entrance from the dining room and glanced at the clock.

He had an hour and a half until he would wake up Chance. Better get another cup of coffee.

Then he peeked into the living room, wanting to see if Lydia went to bed. She hadn't—well, not exactly. She'd gone back to sitting in the lounge chair, which gave her a good view of Brutus and Calvin, but her eyes were closed and her feet propped up in the recliner.

Taking his mug of fresh coffee, he walked through his house, checking the doors and the alarm system. He hoped Lydia was still asleep. He didn't have any more emotional energy left to deal with what was going on between them.

Lydia stood in the entrance to the bistro, the dark shadows slowly evaporating as though the haze was finally lifting from her brain. Part of the restaurant she saw clearly. Melinda standing near the counter with a man she'd seen in the place before. The look on Melinda's face shouted distress, but she kept her voice low. Was the man complaining about an order? Or something else? Her boyfriend?

When Lydia spied tears in Melinda's eyes, she wanted to comfort her friend. The man shoved away from the counter and pivoted toward Lydia. His features less face made her remain in her chair. He came toward her. She tried to see anything—eyes, mouth, nose. Nothing. But he brushed against her, and a chill flash froze her.

Lydia shot straight up in the recliner, her heartbeat pounding in her ears. Her gaze crashed into Jesse's. He sat across from her on the couch.

He rose and came toward her. "What's wrong?"

For a long moment, she couldn't form her words to explain the dream—no, nightmare. "Some guy was arguing with Melinda when I came into the bistro."

"What did he look like?"

"I couldn't see his face. He came right toward me,

but it was blank. That's all I saw, but there was something wrong with that guy."

"What?"

"I don't know." She ground her teeth together. "I've seen him before?"

"Okay. It'll come to you." Jesse sat on the coffee table. "How tall was he?"

Lydia tried to picture the man leaning against the counter, almost in Melinda's face. "Maybe about five-ten."

"What color hair did he have?"

"Brown."

"Long, medium, short?"

"A little long. I saw it sticking out of a ball cap."

"Anything on the ball cap?"

"I don't remember." Frustration churned her stomach. That was all she'd been saying lately.

"Body build?"

Lydia closed her eyes and recalled the faceless man coming toward her. "Lean but not skinny."

"Anything else?"

She shook her head. When she looked at Jesse, there was no reproach in his gaze, only kindness.

"If you just recalled that, you'll remember more. It'll come."

"But in time?"

"This case doesn't hinge on you. You're only one part of it. Thomas is digging into the man who was renting that house. He might have a tie to the bomber. Tomorrow I'll be following up on the pharmacist and visiting the animal shelters about Calvin."

"Can I come? I can't sit home doing nothing."

"Not to the drugstore, but I think it might help if I

take Calvin with me to the shelters. Seeing him might trigger someone's memory, and I know the dog responds to you."

"You're letting me go?"

He cocked a grin. "Besides, it'll take a day for the windows to be replaced in my SUV. I was hoping you would let me borrow your car to use."

She chuckled. "You're sneaky but thanks for letting me help with Calvin. Now that I know that the guy who brought him in is the bomber, I could see him getting a dog from the pound and then poisoning him. But I have an argument about coming to see you with the pharmacist. Seeing him might jar my memory."

"I've got a way for you to watch him from a safe distance. I'll have him come into the station for questioning. He won't see you, but you can see him."

"Thanks." She put the footrest down and stood. "I was going to stay up with you, but obviously I need my sleep. And you should get some, too."

Jesse glanced at his watch. "I have an hour. It'll give me time to think about what we do know so far in this case."

Lydia knelt by the two dogs and reassured herself they were doing well. When she rose, she noticed Jesse had moved back to the couch. After Jesse's response concerning the kiss, she didn't think he was capable of sharing himself with anyone. She had to accept that and quit dreaming they might have a chance after all.

At least she finally had hope that she might recall what she saw in the bistro that would cause the bomber to target her. It had to be that she could identify him. Unlike her relationship with Jesse, which seemed hopeless, it was starting to seem likely that she'd remember…but would it be soon enough?

Lydia sat next to an FBI agent working on the Laughing Bomber Task Force while Thomas and Jesse interviewed Phillip Keats, the pharmacist. Thomas sat across from Phillip, but Jesse was right next to him with Brutus on the man's other side, as if the man were boxed in. When the pharmacist had come into the interrogation room, the dog had sniffed him but didn't indicate anything. Jesse crowded Phillip who leaned as far from Jesse as he could get without getting up and moving his chair.

"I understand you were in the bistro not long before it was bombed. Why didn't you come forward to help us with identifying the people who could be victims?" Thomas asked.

Phillip slid a look toward Jesse, then Brutus. "Am I safe with him not on a leash?"

"He would only attack if I gave the command. You didn't answer the detective's question. Why didn't you come forward?" The fierce expression on Jesse's face even gave Lydia pause.

Phillip swallowed hard. "I don't go in there much and didn't know anyone."

"Ah, that's interesting when you were seen talking to a woman. And from what I understand that woman didn't survive the blast. Didn't you think the police needed to know she was in there?" Thomas's calm voice held only curiosity, not blame.

Sweat coated Phillip's forehead and began rolling down his face. He lowered his head.

Jesse hit his palm against the table. "It's a simple yes or no question."

The pharmacist jumped and leaned even farther away from Jesse. "I couldn't come forward," the man mumbled.

"Why not? You left before her. Why?" Again Thomas's soft tone was meant to calm the man down.

While Phillip wiped his hand across his brow, the FBI agent asked, "Do you remember anything else? Anything that would help with the questions to ask Mr. Keats?"

She shook her head. Something nagged at her, but she couldn't pinpoint it.

Finally Phillip looked right at Thomas. "Okay. I was there with Miss Prince. You knew she was in there. Her name was listed as one of the victims, so what was I going to tell you that you didn't already know?"

"Oh, I don't know. Maybe who else you remember being there? Don't you want us to find the bomber? What if you saw him?" Jesse's taunts made the man wince.

"I don't remember anyone. I was there to see—my friend. That was all. I had limited time before I had to be back at work. I'm not a criminal because I didn't say anything."

"So why didn't you?" Jesse asked.

The pharmacist's eyes grew narrow. "Because I'm a married man."

Thomas wrote something on a pad. "Ah, are you saying you were having an affair with Miss Prince?"

"She was a friend, but someone might mistake us eating lunch together as something more."

"While you were there, did you see anything suspicious?" Jesse snapped his fingers, and Brutus came to his side.

"I saw a man storm out of the bistro after talking to the owner."

Then her dream last night was true. Lydia felt it was but couldn't be sure until now.

Thomas cleared his throat. "I thought you didn't go to the bistro much. How do you know who the owner is?"

"I saw her picture on the news. That bombing was plastered all over the place. Kind of hard to avoid."

"What did the man look like? Is he one of these?" Thomas laid an array of pictures on the table.

"Nope, I don't think so. I never saw his face. I just heard him say something to the owner. I wasn't sitting too far from them."

Lydia leaned forward as Thomas asked, "What?"

"You're going to pay for this."

She'd known the man was angry, but this was a whole new level.

"When did you leave the restaurant?" Jesse asked, pulling the man's attention to him.

The pharmacist shrugged. "I don't remember. I do know I was back at the drugstore when the bomb went off."

"How long?" Jesse fired back.

Phillip sighed. "I… I guess maybe a minute."

"Did you see him leaving?" the FBI agent asked Lydia.

"No. Maybe he left while I was in the bathroom."

"How long were you in the restroom?"

"A few minutes."

When she turned back to the screen, Phillip Keats

was on his feet, looking at his watch. "I have to get to work."

Both Jesse and Thomas rose at the same time and Thomas passed a card to the pharmacist. "If you remember anything later, please call me no matter how unimportant you think it is."

Phillip pocketed it. "Sure. I want this guy caught like everyone else in Anchorage."

Lydia stared at the screen, watching the three leave the interview room. It hadn't triggered her memory, but it had given her an uneasy feeling as though something he said should have sparked a memory of that day. What did the man with Melinda look like?

The FBI agent stood. "Did you remember anything else?"

"No." The answer was just out of her reach. She knew something but couldn't access it. Every time she tried to, her mind shut down. Jesse was right. Forcing her to remember wasn't helping. Other than a nagging feeling, she hadn't gotten anything from the interview.

The FBI agent opened the door for her to go into the hall first. As she emerged, she found Thomas and Jesse with Brutus waiting for her.

"Anything?" Thomas asked.

She shook her head. "I didn't know he was having an affair, and I'm glad he confirmed that Melinda and a man were arguing, but other than that I didn't get anything new."

"Technically, according to Keats, he and Miss Prince were just friends." Jesse smiled at her. "Ready to take Calvin for a ride?"

The warmth in his gaze shored up her flagging spirits. He used to do that when they were dating. Make her feel better. That was one of the many reasons why she fell in love with him. "I'd like to find the man who left Calvin, not only because he's probably the bomber but he poisoned the dog. I hope Calvin is the one who leads us to him. That would be apropos."

Jesse placed his hand at the small of her back and made his way toward the rear exit. As Lydia emerged from the police station, a cool breeze blew, adding a chill to the air. Jesse continued toward her car, surveying the parking lot.

As she unlocked the driver's door, she paused while Jesse had Brutus circle her vehicle and sniff for a bomb and put him in the backseat. She panned the area, goose bumps streaking up her spine as if someone was watching her. Or was it just the fact Brutus had searched for a bomb in her car? She quickly slipped behind the steering wheel. The feeling made her want to lock herself in Jesse's house and never leave until this man was apprehended.

While she started the car, Jesse climbed into the passenger seat. "Is something wrong? You're pale. Did you remember something?"

"Do you always have Brutus do that when you get into a car?"

"Lately, since we began working on the bombing case."

"He's valuable to have around." She pulled out of the parking lot and chalked up the feeling to watching Brutus checking for a bomb.

"Yes. He saved my life yesterday. When I was waiting with Brutus for the ambulance, I thought of Jake Nichols and Mitch. They were both injured critically, but worse, their partnership has come to an end. I've been thinking about that a lot. That could have happened to me and Brutus."

"What would you have done? Have you prepared yourself for that? You've been a partner for six years. Brutus is eight years old."

Jesse blew a long breath out. "I don't think I want to talk about that. The very idea unsettles me, and I need to be sharp to catch this bomber. The idea of losing…" His voice faded into silence.

Lydia slanted a look toward Jesse. "The idea of losing anyone in your life is hard. I've had my share of losses. My mother and dad. My baby daughter." She coated her dry throat. "And I'm afraid I'm losing my sister."

"How have you gotten through it, especially with your child?"

How? And with no support from Aaron. "I used to think the Lord had abandoned me after what happened between Aaron and me. My father certainly let me think that. But now, looking back, I've seen God's hand in my healing. It didn't happen overnight. It's been a long journey, but nothing is forever except for His love. I hope one day to have another child. Actually I hope two."

"Two?"

She decided to be bold. "Do you want to have children?" As teenagers they had never talked about it.

Silence lengthened into minutes.

She should have realized that would shut down their conversation. She turned onto his street.

"Yes. Before I lost my parents, I had a good home life. I want to give that to my child."

She wished he'd said *our* child, but of course he

didn't. As a teenager it had taken him a long time to admit he loved her. Once he did, that was all he would share—the words, not the feelings behind them.

"What happened? Why didn't you ever marry?" She pulled into his garage.

Jesse sat in Lydia's car, staring out the windshield at his wall of tools. He grasped for the words to tell her how he felt as a child and especially after she left Anchorage with Aaron. It went beyond anger and betrayal. He didn't know if he could describe the emptiness he'd experienced.

He angled toward her. "I never found anyone to replace you."

"I've regretted my impulsive actions so much. I've paid for that mistake tenfold. I still love you, Jesse. I don't think I ever stopped loving you."

"And yet, you became pregnant with Aaron's child. It should have been mine." The words tumbled out of his mouth before he could censor them. In that moment, he realized he hadn't forgiven her as he thought.

Her gaze wide, she sucked in a breath.

"I loved you so much. I thought you would be my family. The one I always wanted. Instead you left with Aaron. I... I..." The loneliness he'd fought all his life swamped him.

Tears shone in her eyes. "I'm sorry."

"I know that, and I'm trying to let go of the hurt I felt. So much has been happening lately, I feel like our lives are caught up in a whirlwind and we can't get out of it."

She nodded. "Exactly."

He needed her to understand. She had always accused him of keeping his emotions bottled up and she was right. "When my father went missing in the wilderness, my mother left me with our nearest neighbor who lived a few miles away and went out looking for him. It had been snowing some but nothing bad. The neighbor notified the closest town, and they were going to form a search party, but the weather turned and a blizzard came through. Later they found my mother dead. I still had hope my dad was alive. They both knew how to survive in the wilderness. A week later, his body was discovered, mauled by animals. I was eight and lost everything—home, family and friends. My grandmother wasn't well at all and couldn't take me in. I went into foster care in Anchorage."

She touched his hand. "When my mother walked out on the family, at least my father was there."

He clasped her fingers, needing the connection. "I was supposed to be adopted until the couple found a younger child. After that, I stopped dreaming about a new family. I began to rely on myself only. Then you came into my life, and I started to have hope again."

A tear slipped down her cheek.

His cell phone sounded, and he quickly answered it when he saw it was Thomas.

"The tail I had following Phillip Keats lost him. He didn't show up back at work."

TWELVE

"Thanks for letting me know," Jesse replied and looked at Lydia. He lifted his hand and ran his thumb across her cheek to wipe the tear away.

The gesture sent her pulse racing. "Who was that?"

"Thomas. The detail following Keats lost him."

Again she ran through the scene of seeing him at the table with a woman. She tried to remember when he got up. Did she see him leave? *Please, Lord, I need Your help. What am I forgetting*? "What are we going to do?"

"What we planned. If it's Keats, we need evidence to bring him in. Thomas has a BOLO out on his car as well as staking out the drugstore and his house. Meanwhile Thomas is digging into the man's life." He caressed her cheek one more time. "When this is over with, we'll figure things out."

"I want that." She started to get out of her car.

"Wait. I'll get Calvin. Last night we bonded." He threw her a grin and slid from the front seat.

While he was inside retrieving the American Eskimo, she turned to Brutus and petted him. "How are you doing?"

He barked.

Lydia had assumed he would put Brutus in the house when they came to pick up Calvin, but she realized with Phillip's location unknown he wanted him to check her car each time they returned to it. After Calvin was settled in the backseat with Brutus, she backed out of the garage and drove toward their first destination.

By the fourth one, Lydia tried to keep from being disappointed that no one at the shelters recognized Calvin nor had there been an adoption of an American Eskimo in the past six months. With a sigh, she parked near the entrance.

"I hope this produces a lead, but not all trails we follow lead anywhere. We have to rule this possibility out. For all we know the man had Calvin a long time."

"That makes it even worse that he would give his dog chocolate in order to send the police on a wild-goose chase."

"Let's go. We still have a few more to check. I told Williams to be at the house by one."

"Where are you going after you drop me off?"

"Wherever Thomas sends me. He might have something on Keats by then or the lead on the Chevy behind the appliance store might give us some information."

"What lead?"

"They found the car and Thomas is going to pay the man who owns it a visit. He looks like the sketch of the guy who was in the appliance store. At least his license picture does."

"Who is it?"

"Shane Taylor. Do you know him?"

"No, but I'm glad the police have found him. One of these leads will pan out."

They entered the shelter with both dogs on leashes. Jesse showed his badge and asked to talk to the staff members.

The silver-haired woman came forward. "What's this about?"

"It has to do with an investigation."

Lydia walked a few steps toward the woman. "Have you seen this dog? We believe he was at a shelter, and we need to find his owner."

"He looks a lot like Calvin. He was adopted a few weeks ago." The American Eskimo started wagging his tail and moving toward the older woman. She bent over and stroked him. "Where did you find him? The man who adopted him seemed glad to get him. He wanted a medium-sized dog, and Calvin fit what he was looking for. Calvin's original owner died, and I was hoping he'd find a home, especially because of the owner's sudden death in the church's bombing."

"Was that owner Ed Brown?" Jesse asked.

Surprise lit the manager's eyes. "How did you know?"

"I attend that church, and I knew the people who were killed. Do you have any security tapes of the person who adopted Calvin?"

She shook her head. "This is a small operation. Myself, DJ and a few volunteers are the only ones here usually."

"Can you describe the man?"

The woman tilted her head to the left and tapped the side of her jaw. "Let me see. About six feet. He wore a hoodie, but I believe his hair was blond, not too long."

Lydia recalled the man leaving the bistro had a hoodie on. "What color hoodie?"

"Dark. I think navy blue or black. I'm not sure. I did notice he had beautiful gray eyes though."

"How old do you think he was?" Lydia asked.

The woman lifted her shoulders in a shrug. "I guess thirty or forty."

Jesse pulled up on his cell phone the sketch of the person Lydia ran into going into the bistro. "Does this look like the man who adopted Calvin?"

Her forehead crinkled. "Maybe. I don't know for sure."

Jesse went through the rest of the sketches or photos he had. "Does anyone look familiar to you?"

"No, not really, but I'm not good with faces."

"Did this DJ see the man?" Jesse stuck his phone in his pocket.

"No, he was at lunch. It was only me. The man came just minutes after DJ left."

"Do you have his paperwork? Did he use a credit card or write a check for the adoption fees?"

The older woman shook her head. "Cash. Wait right here. I'll get the paperwork and make a copy of it for you."

"Wait. I need to handle the paper. It's evidence now."

The manager's eyes grew round as she headed into her office. "What did this man do?"

"He's a person of interest in a case."

She pulled out a file cabinet and found what she was looking for.

"I'll need to take your fingerprints to rule out yours on the paper."

"Sure." She passed him the document.

"Did DJ ever handle this?"

"No. He has nothing to do with the paperwork."

While Jesse went to the car to get his fingerprinting kit, Lydia looked around. "How many animals can you take in?"

"Not nearly enough. I have room for thirty and often need to turn away animals."

"Do you work with a vet?"

"Yes, but he's only here from May to September. I need to find another one."

"I'd like to volunteer." Lydia dug her business card from her purse and handed it to the woman. "I can fill in from October to April."

"Bless you. You are an answer to a prayer. Our vet just informed me he was going to start going to Arizona for winters." She stuck out her hand. "By the way, I'm Nadine."

"I'm Lydia."

Nadine glanced at the business card. "Are you related to Robert McKenzie? He was a vet who died last year."

"Yes. He was my father."

"He used to help us out. It's like it's come full circle."

Jesse reentered the office, bagged the adoption paper and fingerprinted Nadine. When they left the shelter, Jesse again had Brutus sniff for a bomb as though it were an everyday routine. But to Lydia, it drove home what was happening.

Lydia put the car in Reverse as he lifted the paper out of the evidence bag by pinching one corner with his gloved fingers. "Guess who adopted Calvin? Sam Alexander."

"The guy you found already dead in the house that exploded."

"Yes. Let's drop the evidence off before going home. We'll have to dig into Alexander's life. He can't be the bomber because he was dead from a drug overdose about two weeks before the bomb went off in his house."

"He could have bombed the hardware store."

"But that would mean someone killed him and continued bombing. Maybe he had a partner and they had a falling-out."

"But why?" Lydia massaged her temples, trying to make sense of what was going on. The Sam Alexander who adopted Calvin had to be wearing a disguise, so he could have been working with the bomber.

"I wish I had an answer to that. Then I would know who was behind all this."

By the time they arrived at the police station, Lydia's head throbbed. Before Kate came home from school she needed to lie down and catch up on the sleep she'd been missing. She wished she could stay in the car while Jesse went inside, but the memory of that feeling of being watched earlier reinforced her fear of being alone.

Lydia lay on the bed at Jesse's house, but no matter how much she wanted and tried to take a nap, she couldn't. It was good to get out for a while today, but she couldn't shake the feeling she was a target with a big, red bull's-eye on her. After listening to Phillip talking with Thomas and Jesse, she'd felt she was missing something. It was inside her mind, locked away, and she couldn't find the key to open it.

Maybe it was the fact she told Jesse she loved him and still everything was unsettled. What had she thought he would do—declare his love back?

She stared at the white ceiling, silence surrounding her. Jesse and Don were in the kitchen the last time she saw them going through the evidence, hoping something would jump out at them. Thomas had come back with the results of the fingerprints on the adoption paper.

No match in the database but Sam Alexander didn't have a record. Thomas had discovered Sam would have had access to the C-4 at his construction job. So it was possible he was tied to the bomber in some way, but sorting through the rubble of his house after the bomb would take a while.

She heard footsteps coming down the hall, and suddenly the door burst open. Kate charged into the room and flounced onto the bed, letting her backpack slip to the floor.

"Did something go wrong at school?" Lydia prepared herself for an onslaught of anger.

"Connor. When I left today, I saw him talking to Mandy and they disappeared down the hallway." Kate twisted toward her. "He gets tired of me telling him I can't do anything. He can't even come over here. You've made it plain he isn't welcome."

Here, it comes. It's all my fault.

Kate chewed on her bottom lip. "I don't think he cares about me as much as he says he does. We had a big fight about me not being able to see him after school. Why would he go with Mandy? I tried calling him. He didn't answer." Tears began streaming down her sister's face.

Lydia sat up and scooted toward Kate. "I'm sorry. If he can't understand why you can't be there right now after school, then maybe he isn't the boy for you."

"He should know. He was here the other day and knows what's happening to you."

"It can be hard to put yourself in another's shoes. Maybe he knows on some level, but doesn't really get it."

Kate pulled out her phone. "All I can say is he better text me. Soon." She knuckled the tears away and rose, heading for the hallway.

There was a part of Lydia that would love to relive her senior year, so she could undo what had gone wrong. But there was a part that was so glad she wasn't a teenager anymore, especially as she saw what Kate was going through.

She reclined back on the bed. Thoughts of Connor and Kate arguing morphed into visions of the dream she'd had about Melinda arguing with her boyfriend. *It was her boyfriend, I remember that now. But why can't I see what he looks like? What did Melinda tell me after they talked?*

Then a faded image materialized in her mind. Shadowy. Down at the end of the hall at the bistro, hand on doorknob. He glanced back at her and she met his— cold, gray eyes. That was all she could see. What did he look like? Why was he leaving the restaurant that way?

She lay there for a while longer, but nothing else appeared—a vague person with gray eyes. Was it the man she ran into as she came into the bistro? If so, why was he in the hallway?

Exasperated, she pushed to a sitting position. She felt as though she were going crazy. Bits and pieces of information floating around in her mind, but nothing came together into a whole picture. People's lives depended on her remembering.

A dark screen fell over her thoughts and shut everything out.

Frustrated, she stood and decided to find Jesse. She needed a distraction.

As she walked through the living room, Kate sat on the couch talking to Connor. She lowered her voice as Lydia made her way into the kitchen.

Jesse looked up at her and grinned. "Thomas discovered that Sam Alexander had an older man visit him several times in the past month and that Alexander did get a dog but it hasn't been seen in a while."

"Who? How did he find out?" Lydia sat across from Jesse with Don next to her.

"From the neighbor who wasn't home. This morning Thomas was able to talk to the couple before they left for work."

"What did the older man look like?" Lydia hoped this would lead to the bomber.

Jesse's smile grew. "That's the best part. The husband identified him from the sketch of the man with Calvin at the animal hospital, except according to the neighbor, this 'Mr. Jacobs' didn't have a limp and could get around with no problem."

Moving like a younger man. Lydia could see why Jesse was excited. They were getting closer to the bomber and his true identity. "So he called him Mr. Jacobs?"

"No. He didn't know the man's name. Thomas checked with some of the other neighbors and another said they had seen an older man come and go from Alexander's house. This past month or so."

"So do you two think the bomber got his C-4 from Sam?" Lydia looked from Don to Jesse.

"Maybe. Thomas is coming over to fill us in on a couple of other developments." Jesse studied her for a few seconds. "Leads are starting to produce some results."

The doorbell rang, and Don hurried to answer it.

"You okay?" Jesse held her hand. "Mary told Williams when she escorted Kate to the house that she was extremely upset when Mary picked her up at school."

"Boyfriend problems. Connor wants her to spend more time with him."

"Since he's been here already, he could come over after school, on the weekends, if you think that will make things easier."

The more she saw of Connor the more Lydia likened him to Aaron. She prayed her sister didn't do something stupid like she had. When she'd tried to have a conversation with her sister about sex, Kate shut her down. Dad had already given her the talk, and she didn't intend to go through that embarrassing subject again.

Lydia rolled her shoulders to ease the tension setting in. "Frankly, I'm glad he's showing his true colors to Kate. He has a one-track mind, and I know he's been pushing Kate to do things that—"

"That you did when you were a teenager," Kate said from the doorway.

Lydia closed her eyes for a few seconds, then twisted in the chair to look at Kate. "Yes. I know firsthand the mistake it was."

"He called and explained that Mandy's locker was stuck, and he helped her get it open. That was all."

Don and Thomas came up behind Kate, and she stepped out of the entrance, disappearing around the corner into the living room. Probably to call or text Connor again. Lydia heaved a heavy sigh.

Thomas took the chair Don had used while the officer left to check outside. The detective slid the sketch to Lydia. "This is the sketch Nadine gave us of Sam Alexander. It fits the driver's license for that man. He worked in construction. The AFT agent is interviewing his employer about the C-4, but I've got a feeling some is missing."

Lydia's gaze fixed on the young man who was found in a freezer in the bombed rental house. "So you think he supplied the C-4 to the bomber and that guy killed him so he couldn't identify him?"

"They could have been partners for the first bomb and had a falling-out," Thomas said.

Jesse took a look at the sketch. "Or, maybe Alexander blackmailed the bomber after the first bomb went off."

Thomas frowned. "The descriptions of the person we think might be the bomber are different each time. Remember that couple out walking on the street where the church was, not five minutes before the bomb went off? They saw a guy wearing a hoodie, slender build. And on the traffic cam near the hardware store, a person we think was the bomber leaving the scene before the explosion early that morning had a hoodie but a potbelly. Physical body type keeps changing as well as facial features and coloring."

Lydia sat forward. "Hoodie? Like the guy I ran into

as I went into the bistro. We collided as he left and he was wearing a hoodie."

Jesse captured her gaze. "Did he have a potbelly?"

"I'm not sure. I think he was what I would call husky. Did the couple see the color of his eyes? The guy at the bistro had gray ones."

"No, he had on sunglasses even though it was starting to get dark." Thomas huffed. "We have thin, fat, old, young. Gray hair, dark hair."

"If the couple saw the bomber, then why didn't he come after them like he is with me?"

Jesse snapped his fingers. "That's it. You saw the real bomber. The others were disguises—someone who knew how to apply makeup and play a role convincingly."

"Okay, why the bistro?" Flashes of the fractured memories from that day paraded through her mind.

"Not sure. We may not have the bomber on that traffic cam and the couple might not have seen the guy doing this. But the person who brought Calvin in has to be the bomber." Thomas stood. "But in disguise."

"What about Shane Taylor and the black Chevy? What did you find out there? What does he look like?" Jesse rose and went to the coffeepot to refill his mug.

"He was like what the salesman in the appliance store described, and he has an alibi for the first two bombings. He said he was there looking for a washing machine." As Thomas paced in a circle he looked at Lydia. "We're getting close. Hang in there. Well, I've taken a long enough break."

Lydia chuckled. "You call this a break. You're going to need a month's vacation when this is over with."

"Let us know what you find out about the C-4." Jesse walked with Thomas toward the foyer.

Was the gray-eyed stranger she'd bumped into the bomber? And who was the man using the hallway exit?

So many questions and so few answers.

When Jesse returned and sat in the chair next to Lydia, she told him about the faceless person with gray eyes who haunted her. "I can't shake him. But I know the pharmacist has brown eyes. I can't picture who was fighting with Melinda yet, and the guy who left the bistro as I came in had gray eyes. And I'm sure the old man with Calvin had blue eyes. They misted with tears when he wasn't sure Calvin would make it. How reliable are my memories? They seem so disjointed."

"Contact lenses can change a person's eye color." Jesse stroked his hand down her arm, the gesture meant to reassure her.

What would happen when this was over? Lydia didn't want to think about that question. "I forgot to ask if Thomas ever found Phillip Keats. Did he find him?"

"Yes, he showed up at the drugstore around one with some story that he went for a drive to clear his head. At least that's what he told a coworker."

"I guess it's a good thing he's part owner. A lot of bosses would fire someone over that."

"I kind of know what Keats feels like. I would like to clear my head."

"So would I. I keep getting brief images, and I can't tell what's real anymore. If only the bomber knew I have no idea who he is, he would leave me alone."

Jesse pulled her toward him. "You're trying too hard."

"I know you keep telling me that. Then I get a dirty look from Kate because of what's going on and—"

He laid two fingers over her lips. "Shh. Don't tell Thomas, but this evening let's not think about the bomber or the bombings. A deal?"

"Sounds wonderful. Although I'm not sure I'll be able to do it."

"Tell you what. My SUV is ready. After dinner you can drive me to get it, then I'll follow you back here and we can go for a ride. Just you and me."

"I don't think—"

"You're thinking too hard. I'm thinking too hard. I believe it'll help us. Let's go to Point Woronzof and see the sun set. Okay?"

"I haven't been there since we were teenagers."

"Then it's a date."

A date? Casually said, but it sparked memories. And here she was, still in love with Jesse. How was she going to deal with real life when the bomber was caught?

Leaving the parking lot at Point Woronzof, Jesse held Brutus's leash in one hand and Lydia's in the other as they made their way carefully down the hillside to the small-pebbled beach. Glacial silt tinted the waves gray as they washed up onto shore.

Lydia stopped and turned in a full circle. "I'd forgotten how beautiful this view of Cook Inlet and Mount Susitna are."

"I've seen some glorious sunsets from here."

"Yeah, I remember."

As the sun started disappearing behind the mountain line across the inlet, Jesse recalled the first time he'd known he was in love with Lydia. It was the summer before their senior year in high school. They had a picnic dinner at this point and waited for the sun to go down. He'd wanted to tell her how he felt. He could never get the words out and didn't until they reconnected after she'd dated Aaron. At the time, he didn't realize it wouldn't make any difference. She eloped with Aaron not long after. Why did he suggest bringing her here?

Because while they were here, the world hadn't intruded and a feeling of peace pervaded, at least for a short time. They needed that right now, especially in the midst of all that was happening in Anchorage.

"Look. Do you see the whale?" Excitement flowed from Lydia as she moved closer to the water. "Seeing one never ceases to make me smile. They're so beautiful. The Lord has created a whole bunch of unique and fascinating animals."

He pointed to a bald eagle flying above. "Like that one. Majestic."

The joy in her expression spread through him as though it were contagious and for a moment it erased the tragedy and pain in their past and replaced it with the hope only the Lord could give them.

Jesse unhooked Brutus's leash and gave him the signal to play. His dog sniffed his surroundings, exploring a piece of driftwood on the beach.

Then as if to confirm Jesse's thoughts, the sky deepened to a rich orange golden color as the sun dropped behind the mountains. The peace he sought descended while the ravens performed their aerial tricks.

Jesse slipped his arms around Lydia and pulled her back against him. He rested his chin on the top of her head, smelling the apple scent in her shampoo. A memory from his childhood wound its way through his thoughts, bringing a smile to his lips. His mother had pulled an apple pie out of the oven and put it on a cold burner to cool. The aroma from the pie had filled the whole house. He'd started to pinch off a piece of the hot pie. His mom had quickly pulled him back and warned him of the hot plate, but she'd wrapped her arms around him, much as he now held Lydia, and hugged him.

Lydia twisted toward him and locked gazes with him. "Why are you sad?"

He hadn't realized that his expression revealed his sadness. The older he became, the dimmer his thoughts of his childhood with his parents became. He wanted to keep them close always. "The scent of your hair reminded me of my mother when she used to bake us an apple pie. I loved them. Now I can't eat a piece."

"Because the smell brings back the thoughts of losing her?"

He nodded. Since Lydia had come back into his life, he'd done way too much thinking about his past.

Lydia brushed back a wayward strand of hair caught in the brisk breeze. "My mother didn't die. She left us, but I kept wondering for years what did I do to make her go away."

"And?"

"Finally my dad sat me down and explained I didn't do anything wrong. She hated Alaska. Didn't want to be a wife and mother. For a while after that I was so angry with her for leaving. Then again Dad asked me why I was so angry. I told him, and he said to me as long as I hold on to the anger I'll never be totally free to enjoy life. I needed to forgive my mother."

"Did you?"

"Yes. I have no idea where she is, but our family never moved. If she wanted to get hold of Kate and me, she knows where we are. Are you angry at your parents for dying?"

His arms slid away from her, and he stepped back. He wanted to say, no. But he couldn't. "My mother went looking for my dad. Why didn't she wait until the search was organized? She went out alone. She knew better." He glanced to the colors in the sky morphing into a darker orange-red. "So, yes, I guess I have been. She left me with a neighbor and never looked back. That was the last time I saw her."

"You know we both dealt with loss at a young age. Yours was more life changing than mine, but I still feel like I can relate to what you went through."

She was right. Instead of pulling away from her, he should be drawing closer. She knew what he'd gone through. What was stopping him? He took a step toward her.

The loud sound of a large jet flying over them disrupted the moment.

He glanced around at the dusk beginning to settle over the area. "I guess life intrudes. We better head back. It's getting dark."

She remained still, clasping his hand. "I know what you went through as a child. Remember that." Then she gave him a peck on his cheek before starting for the parking lot.

He called Brutus and hooked his leash, then trailed after Lydia, unable to forget her words just now and her dad's advice about letting the anger go. He'd never told anyone he'd been mad at his mother for going out and looking for his dad alone. Lydia was entangling her life into his again, and the thought scared him.

Later that night another dream awakened Lydia, her face drenched in sweat. She knew what happened between Melinda and her boyfriend, Todd, at the bistro. She glanced at Kate sleeping and knew she wasn't going back to sleep for a while. She pulled on some comfortable clothes and crept from the bedroom to seek whoever was on guard. She didn't think she would forget the dream, but she didn't want to take a chance.

In the living room Jesse held a mug, probably with coffee in it, and peeked out the side of the blackout blinds. He looked toward her while Brutus remained asleep on the couch.

She chuckled. "He must not be too concerned about me being up."

"He's been working hard lately. Why are you up? Something wrong?"

"No, but I remembered something from the bistro."

Jesse turned from the window and closed the space between them. "What?"

"I remember the man Melinda was arguing with. It was for sure her boyfriend. They'd been dating for a month. She was at the end of the counter with him. When he stormed away from her, Melinda had an angry expression on her face." Relief washed over Lydia now that she'd told another person.

"Where did he go?"

"I don't know. He walked past my table, but I was trying not to stare."

"What did he look like? Can you give our sketch artist a description? Do you know his last name?"

"He had a black ball cap on with jeans and a blue T-shirt. Brown hair and gray eyes. He went right by me. I'd seen him one other time in the bistro a week before."

"Do you remember anything on the cap? A logo? Something that might help us ID him?"

She shook her head. "No, I was focused on his furious look. I can give a description of him for a sketch. Melinda only referred to him as Todd. A few days earlier when I picked up some food for everyone at work, Melinda had just gotten off the phone with him. I tried to comfort her. They must have been having some problems." Lydia thought back to that day. "The only thing she said was that maybe having a boyfriend wasn't all that it was cracked up to be. She didn't say anything else. The part I'm excited about is he had gray eyes. I keep seeing gray eyes. That's got to mean something." At least she prayed it did.

"Yes. We'll dig into Melinda's personal life and see if we can discover who this boyfriend is."

"I remember two guys with gray eyes. Maybe it was one of them."

"We don't know a lot about the man you ran into when you came in. We know he got into a truck but mud covered the license plate. We have a couple of people searching the traffic cams around town to see if they can catch it." His thumb caressed her face under her eye. "You need to go back to sleep."

"Do I look that bad?"

"On the contrary. You look great, but our lives aren't ours right now. Not until this bomber is found."

She smiled, the reassurance in his touch comforting her. This situation would come to an end, and she would get her life back. "The worst part is, I'm bored. I'm not even at my own house where I could at least clean and organize things."

"Go right ahead. Feel free to do that here."

She laughed. "That's okay. Although I am thinking of cooking a special dinner tomorrow. How about my made-from-scratch meatballs and spaghetti? It was my grandmother's recipe. No sauce out of a bottle. I won't go as far as she did and make my own spaghetti."

"You're making me hungry at two o'clock in the morning. If you need me to pick up any ingredients, just make me a list and I can get them before I start working on the case."

"Is there a chance I can come with you? You know that boredom thing."

Their easy bantering ended as he firmed his mouth and stiffened. "No. Remember what happened at Sam Alexander's house."

"But—"

"End of discussion."

"I got to go to the shelters with you."

"That's because Calvin knows you and responds to you better than me. I'm not taking you to a grocery store where you could be an easy target."

"I could argue the point—" he opened his mouth to say something, and she hurried to finish "—but I'm not going to. I don't want to distract you from your job." She spun on her heel and headed for her bedroom to the sounds of his chuckles.

While Don and Mary played a game of checkers at the kitchen table, Lydia finished up her homemade spaghetti sauce before she turned to making the meatballs.

She would brown them and add them to the sauce. She'd already beat both officers and declared herself the checkers champion. Now they were deciding the runner-up.

Her cell phone rang. She glanced at the screen. Jesse. She quickly wiped her hands off and answered it. "Tell me you've solved the case," she said as she walked into the living room for some privacy.

"I wish I could. I did find out Todd's last name, and I'm heading to his apartment right now."

Her grasp on the phone tightened. "Be careful. He has a temper and could be the bomber."

"I'll have backup. Thomas is working on a lead on the guy you ran into as you entered the bistro. One of the traffic cams found him turning into a housing development. So this is all good news. If they have to, they will go door-to-door to find the truck. They already checked on black trucks of that make and no license plates had addresses in the subdivision, but that doesn't mean he isn't there or working there."

"I love your optimism. Come home hungry. I've made a ton of spaghetti sauce and asked Don and Mary to dinner. They both said yes. I hope we have something to celebrate tonight."

"So do I, but unless one of them confesses, it will take a lot of police work to get the evidence to convict the bomber."

When she hung up, she stood to the side of the picture window and peeked outside between the blind slats. She didn't want to scan the street blatantly and make herself a target, but she probably did this several times an hour. Would she ever stop looking over her shoulder?

She started for the kitchen when her phone rang again. This time it was the school. She hurried and answered it. Kate had been so upset when she went to class this morning.

"Dr. McKenzie, this is Kate's principal."

She hoped her sister didn't get into a fight. "Yes?"

"Kate didn't go to her class after lunch. We've looked everywhere in the building but can't find her."

"Someone kidnapped her?" Hysteria wormed its way through her.

"All outside doors are locked. You have to use the main entrance, and it's monitored so I don't see how that could have happened."

"I'm coming up there, and I'm calling the police." Lydia hit the end button.

Her hands trembled as she punched in Jesse's number and waited for what seemed like an eternity for him to answer. Before he could say hello, Lydia said, "Kate is missing at school. I'm going up there."

"No. Stay with Williams and Collins. I'll take care of finding her and figure out what happened. You said she was upset this morning. Could she be hiding?"

"I don't know what my sister is thinking anymore. The school is locked down and the principal is sure someone didn't come in and take her but…"

"Lydia, I'll handle this. Let the officers know and have them be extra vigilant."

"Okay." But when she finished talking with Jesse, she sank down on a chair nearby, the trembling spreading through her whole body. She didn't know if she could even walk into the kitchen.

This whole mess had been hard enough for *her*, let alone a teenage girl. Maybe she should take Kate to Oklahoma until they found the bomber. She could probably leave without the man finding—

The phone ringing again disrupted her thoughts. She quickly answered, thinking it was Jesse. "Did you hear something?"

"I heard your sister was kidnapped and the bomber has her," a chilling voice said, followed by hideous laughter.

THIRTEEN

Numb, Lydia nearly dropped her phone. "Who is this?"

The same laughter she heard right before the bomb went off assaulted her ears. "You know who this is, and I have your sister. Have you told the police who I am?"

"No, because I don't know."

"Maybe not now. You'll figure it out eventually. I can't have that. I'll let your sister go if you take her place. She hasn't seen my face, but you have. If I see any police around when we make the trade, I'll blow her up. You hold her life in your hands."

"Where do I go?" Lydia asked, a knot jamming her throat.

He gave her a location of a warehouse. "It's abandoned, and I'll know if you tell the police."

Had he bugged Jesse's house like hers? She scanned the living room, feeling as though she was being watched this very second. "I need to talk to Kate."

"Such a demanding person. Remember it's easy for me to set off a bomb. I've done four so far."

Another blast of repulsive laughter petrified her. She couldn't string two words together. She swallowed hard, trying to push the fear down so she could do this.

"Don't make me do a fifth one. When you get to the warehouse, I'll give you a call for further instruction. Here's your sister."

"Lydia, I'm so sorry."

She didn't have to see her sister to know that tears were streaking down her face. "You're going to be all right."

"Please—"

"That's all. You don't have much time. Be here in an hour. Don't let your bodyguards know anything. I know you have two sitting with you right now."

He *had* bugged the house! No, probably just watching it. "I'll be there."

"Don't even think about telling your boyfriend. I can be vindictive if you cross me." The bomber hung up.

The cell phone slipped from her hand and fell onto her lap.

She looked around frantically. She couldn't let her sister die because of her. The man was after her, not Kate. *Lord, what do I do? How do I get out without Don and Mary knowing?*

"Lydia, do you want to play another checkers game? I beat Don," Mary said from the kitchen, her voice sounding as if she was walking toward the living room.

Lydia moved quickly, snatching up her phone and sticking it into her jeans pocket as she stood. She schooled her face into a mask of calm while inside she shook from head to toe.

"Your spaghetti sauce smells wonderful," Mary said as she came into the living room.

Turned away from the officer, she inhaled a deep breath, then swung around. "Thanks. I was telling Jesse you two are staying for dinner tonight. I'm going to let the sauce simmer for an hour while I lie down. Getting up in the middle of the night is wreaking havoc on my sleeping schedule."

"I know what you mean. Do you want me to wake you up in an hour?"

"Yes. Please." Because by then she planned to be at the warehouse.

Once her sister was let go, she intended to fight for her life.

"Thanks." Lydia walked out of the room at a normal pace. When she was out of sight, she disabled the house's alarm system and rushed down the hallway to her bedroom.

After calling for a cab to meet her at the corner, she stuck her car keys into her pocket with some money, then went to her medical bag and prepared a syringe with a heavy-duty tranquilizer that she hoped to use on the bomber. She should be able to conceal it in her long-sleeve T-shirt. She would save her sister and not go down easily.

Please, Lord, let this work.

She hurriedly scribbled a note to Jesse about what was happening and left it for Mary to find. She couldn't risk saying anything before her sister was freed, but by the time Mary found the note, Kate should be safe.

She moved to the window on the side of the house, unlocked it and raised it up. The screen popped out with a little encouragement from her, and she lowered herself to the ground. Without looking back, she ran for the end of the street and prayed the cab would be there soon. When she reached the corner, it wasn't. She paced, checking her watch every moment. Finally after five minutes passed, she pulled her phone from her pocket to call the cab company. She punched in the first three numbers when she spied a taxi coming toward her.

She chewed on her thumbnail while she watched it approach. Once the driver took her to her house, she would take her dad's car, which was stored in the garage.

The cab stopped a few feet from her. "Did you call for a taxi?"

"Yes." She climbed into the back and gave him her address. "I'll double the fare if you'll get there as fast as possible."

When she arrived at her place, she paid the driver, raced into the house and found the keys to the Buick. In the garage, she turned her key. A grinding noise filled the air. It hadn't been driven in weeks, she suddenly realized. The car wouldn't start. What now?

Several K-9 teams were scouring the high school after the dogs sniffed a sweater in Kate's locker as well as her backpack. Jesse covered the area from the girl's last class before lunch. Brutus trailed her scent to a side door. He went outside and followed his dog to the parking lot. He stopped at an empty space.

She left and got into a car? Forcibly? Or on her own?

He hurried back into the building and strode to the principal's office. He'd met the man when he first came fifteen minutes ago. "Mr. Carver, are students allowed to go off campus to eat lunch?"

"No. That would be a security nightmare."

"I traced Kate to the parking lot from her last class.

She went out a side door. I need to know whose car she got into."

"We have monitors on the parking lot. I can pull up the video feed and see if it caught anything."

Five minutes later, Jesse discovered that Kate had gone with Connor off campus and neither one had returned. "I need to talk to some of Kate's and Connor's closest friends. Maybe they know what the pair were doing."

When Jesse interviewed a couple of Kate's friends, no one knew where she'd gone today, although the day before they'd snuck off campus and eaten at Bud's Hamburger Joint. Jesse sent an officer to check in case they went back to the same place.

The next student Jesse talked to was one of Connor's buddies. Quinn came into the principal's office with a closed look on his face.

"Quinn, we discovered that both Kate and Connor are missing from their classes after lunch. I know they left campus. I need to know where they went."

Quinn dropped his gaze to the table. "Don't know."

"You may not be aware, but Kate is being protected by the police because her sister is a witness in the third bombing. I'm concerned something has happened to both of them, so if you know anything you might be saving their lives if you tell me."

The teenager looked at Jesse. "Connor doesn't live far from here. He took her to his house. They probably lost track of time. I was at the door to let them back in, but they didn't show up. I figure they decided to cut this afternoon."

Jesse stood. "Thank you. We'll check it out. What is Connor's address?"

Quinn wrote it on a piece of paper. "They'll be okay, right?"

"I hope so." But he didn't have a good feeling about this.

After getting Connor's address, Jesse left the others to continue searching the high school. He thought about calling Lydia to let her know where Kate went but decided he would wait until he had Kate under his protection. He tried not to think of why the two went to Connor's house. Lydia already had enough problems. This would add to them.

When he pulled into the driveway behind Connor's car, he and Brutus approached the house. He'd get Kate and take her to Lydia. He figured she would want to see her with her own eyes. He would have a few words to say to the boy later.

He rang the doorbell, and when no one came to the door, he peered into the front window. He tried the door. Locked. The car was still there so they had to be inside. He strode around the house, looking into every window he could. From a back window he saw Connor on the floor, not moving. There was no sign of Kate.

In her haste, Lydia had flooded the engine. After sitting for a while, the car started and she backed out of her garage, praying she still had time to save Kate.

As Lydia drove toward the warehouse, the bomber called again. He told her to toss her cell phone out the window. At the warehouse there would be a phone that couldn't be traced. She had no intention of doing that. She could be tracked with the signal.

Her phone rang again. She didn't answer it. After a second call, she received a text from the bomber and pulled over to the curb. I know you haven't done what I said. Throw it out now or your sister dies.

He must be following her. She scanned her surrounding but couldn't tell where he might be. A few cars passed her. Was he in one of them? She had no choice. She flung the cell out the window and continued her journey to the warehouse.

Lydia approached her destination and drove around back. After parking where he had told her to, she looked for the cell and found it, then sat in her car to wait.

Five minutes passed before the cell phone rang. She snatched it from her lap and said, "Where do I go now?"

"Drive down to the warehouse at the end of the row. Then I'll let you know."

She followed his directions and again waited. This time it was ten minutes before she received another call.

"Go to the back door of the warehouse on the left. It'll be unlocked. Go inside and wait."

As she headed for the building, she wondered if it was another stall tactic. Would she be sent somewhere else? If only she could remember who the bomber was and why he wanted her dead. The two cooks who survived in the bistro kitchen hadn't been targeted. She had seen him in the dining room. But who?

Then a vision of the gray eyes filled her mind, but this time the face became clearer. It wasn't gray eyes she saw but reflective sunglasses he put on right before he went out the bistro's exit door at the end of the hallway to the restrooms.

Her hand shook as she opened the door to the abandoned building. Inside, she paced in a circle, afraid to go too far into the cavernous area. She looked into the dim shadows surrounding her. Was he here now—watching her? Her heartbeat raced so fast she felt light-headed. She inhaled deeply, then exhaled to calm herself as much as possible.

The man leaving the bistro wearing the sunglasses had glanced back when she went into the bathroom and she'd looked right at him for three seconds. Then he'd hurriedly left.

A movement to the right in the warehouse caught Lydia's attention. A man stepped out of the darkness. She gasped. "It's you."

After calling Thomas, Jesse picked the lock on the front door, then entered with gun drawn and Brutus off his leash, sniffing as he went. Jesse checked each room while he worked his way back to where the teenager was. He wouldn't put it past the bomber to have a repeat of what happened at Sam Alexander's place. When Sam's body was found in a freezer, it was determined he'd been dead for weeks. Jesse prayed that Connor wasn't dead and there wasn't a bomb ready to explode. He had to find Kate for Lydia.

When Jesse went into the teenager's bedroom, he hurried toward the boy while Brutus searched the area. He checked for a pulse and found one. As he called for an ambulance, he surveyed Connor, whose legs and hands were tied behind his back, to see the extent of his injuries. All he found was a head wound with matted blood around it. More had pooled on the floor. He untied Connor.

While waiting for the ambulance and Thomas, he scanned the room as Brutus went from one object to the next, sniffing. If the bomber was the one who did this, at least he left the teenager alive, but he must have taken Kate. They would have to assume that was the case and start canvassing the street for any information. They could look at traffic cams, but they needed an idea of what kind of vehicle the bomber drove. And they needed to know fast.

Connor stirred on the floor, his eyes blinking open. Obviously disoriented, he stared at Jesse for a moment, tried to move and groaned.

"An ambulance is on its way. I wouldn't move. You were hit on the head. Do you remember what happened?"

Connor tried to sit up and collapsed back against the floor. Jesse caught him before he hit his head. "Where's Kate?"

"He must…" Connor's hoarse voice gave out.

"She's not here. Who is he?" Jesse kept his voice calm as panic descended over Connor's features, his eyes rounding as he tried to get up again and could barely lift his head. Jesse held him still.

"Did he…" Connor opened his mouth, but no words came out for a few seconds then he continued, "…take her?"

"Kate is missing. Who is *he*?"

"He burst in here as we…" Connor averted his gaze.

"If Kate has been kidnapped, we need to know everything now. Time is of the essence."

"He moved so fast." Connor paused for a few seconds, closing his eyes.

Jesse thought he might have lost consciousness again.

But Connor continued. "He had a bat…he knocked me out."

"So you don't know who tied you up?"

"No." Connor opened his eyes.

"What did he look like?" Jesse asked as the sound of sirens grew louder.

"Wore a ski mask."

"Do you remember anything about him?"

"About my size." Connor sucked in a breath. "I heard Kate scream… He took her?"

"I'm assuming he did. She isn't here."

"Is he the bomber?"

"I think so. Anything you can tell me would be great."

Connor's eyes slid closed again. The teen might not be much help at this time, but maybe the house could tell him something.

As the paramedics came down the hall, Connor's eyes popped open. "He wore black. Even black gloves."

Thomas followed the paramedics into the bedroom. Jesse stood and made his way to him. "All he could tell me was the man was about his size and wore black. He had on a ski mask and used gloves so I doubt there are prints."

"Do you know how he got in?"

"I think he picked one of the locks on an outside door. That's how I got into the house when I saw the kid on his floor."

"Brutus checked for a bomb?"

"First thing. None of us, including my dog, wants a repeat of the other day. My body is still healing."

"I think the best use of our manpower right now is

to go house to house and see if anyone saw something. Have you called Lydia?"

"I was going to after you all came."

"Not a call you want to make?" Thomas's mouth twisted in a frown.

"No. She's going to blame herself. This wouldn't have happened if Kate hadn't left school. But in Lydia's mind it will become her fault *her* sister is in danger. I'll also call Connor's parents. I'll get the contact information from school."

"Tell her it's the bomber's fault." Thomas left to organize a door-to-door canvas of the neighbors at home.

The first task Jesse did was to inform Connor's parents about what happened at their house and where their son was being taken. Finally he had no choice but to call Lydia. If he wasn't needed here to help find Kate, he'd rather tell her in person, but that wasn't an option. He let her phone ring until it went to voice mail. She hadn't slept well last night. She must be taking a nap.

He gave Williams a call, and the officer answered on the second ring. "Is Lydia asleep?"

"Yeah."

"How long?"

"An hour. Mary was about to wake her up."

"We haven't found Kate, but we know some of what happened. I need to tell her."

"Kate is missing?"

Jesse gripped his cell phone tighter. "She called me about Kate being gone when the school called her. She was supposed to tell you."

"She didn't say anything to me or Mary."

Why didn't Lydia tell the officers guarding her?

His gut knotted. Something was wrong. "Kate went to her boyfriend's house at lunch. It seems yesterday and today they sneaked off campus. The doors are locked to prevent people from coming into the building but not going out. I found Connor knocked out and Kate gone. A man in black came in and took her. As much as I hate it, you need to wake Lydia up."

"I'm making my way to her bedroom now."

Jesse heard Williams knock on the door. There was a long pause, then another knock, louder this time.

"She's not answering. I'm going inside," Williams said as Jesse heard a slight creaking sound as he opened the door. "The window is open. She's gone."

Jesse went cold. "I'm on my way. Check the whole house and let me know what you find."

"Where's Kate?" Lydia stared at the bomber dressed in black, not ten feet from her.

"Somewhere safe and alive."

"And why should I believe you?"

"Because you don't have a choice, if you want your sister to live. I have no issue with Kate, but I do with you. I know you were remembering. I could tell by the direction of the police investigation, but mostly from the bug I placed in Calvin's dog collar. I didn't think you were going to take him home with you. That was a bonus. I just hoped to get some info when the police realized the bomber brought the animal in."

"Calvin could have died."

He shrugged. "You could ID me. I took care of the waitress who served me. If you'd died like you were supposed to, I'd have stopped. Now I'll have to set off another bomb just to throw the police off. They need to think it's a lunatic who is doing this."

He was a lunatic. Anyone who did what he had done wasn't in his right mind. "Why are you setting off bombs?"

"Because I had to kill my girlfriend. She purposely got pregnant with my child. She actually thought I would leave my wife. She's coming into a lot of money soon when her father's estate is finally settled. I've stayed married to her for years. I'm not walking away from all that wealth now."

What a sicko! Lydia pressed the arm with the syringe against her side. Somehow if her plan was to work, she had to get close to him. Once she tranquilized him, she could tie him up with the rope she brought from her house and call the police. Then he wouldn't be able to set off any more bombs, and she and Kate would be safe.

"So you killed all those people to cover up one death." She couldn't keep the contempt from her voice.

He ignored her statement and said, "Toss the phone to me."

She did as instructed but hit him in the chest hard, then whirled around and ran for the door. She wanted him to come after her, but she had to make it look like she was genuinely fleeing. As she raced toward the exit, she lowered the syringe so one end was cupped in her palm. Then she stumbled on purpose and went down, using the commotion to free the shot completely.

He grabbed her and jerked her to her feet. "Stupid woman. If you escape, I'll just have to kill your sister."

Before he had a chance to push her forward, she lunged at him and stabbed the needle into his upper arm. He backhanded her, sending her flying into the door. When she struck it, all the air whooshed from her lungs.

He took a step toward her. She'd given him enough tranquilizer to put a horse down. He kept coming toward her, but he weaved from side to side.

It had to work.

He stopped in front of her, his eyelids sliding closed. As she fumbled for the door handle, he put his hands around her neck and squeezed.

As Jesse drove toward his house with Brutus, he put a call in to headquarters to track her cell phone.

He was turning into his driveway when he received a call about the location of the phone. He ran to his house to get the two officers and grab something with Lydia's scent on it. Then he headed toward the location he'd been given. The signal was stationary. He tried to think what was in that location. Not a house—it wasn't residential. A building?

He reached the short street and pulled over to the curb. A vacant lot stood where the cell signal was emanating. Not a good sign. "We need to find the phone. Maybe there's something on it that can help us."

Jesse let Brutus out of the rear of the SUV and let him smell the sweater. "Find."

When his K-9 sat and looked at him, Jesse hurried over. The cell phone was hidden in the tall weeds. He put on a pair of gloves and looked at the calls she'd received recently. When he read the text message, he figured the phone would be a dead end, but he called headquarters to see if the number of the person who called her last could be traced. While he waited, he surveyed the street. Not the best part of town.

After he received the call informing him the cell couldn't be traced, he turned to the two patrol officers. "We need to check around here to see if anyone saw her."

But as each minute ticked by, Jesse couldn't forget the words, "Throw it out now or your sister dies."

In that moment he realized he might lose the woman he loved.

Before Lydia had a chance to knee the pharmacist, his hands slipped from around her neck as he swayed on his feet, then crumbled to the concrete floor. She shoved him to the side, opened the door and ran to her car for the rope. When she came back to the warehouse, she retrieved his cell phone and called Jesse.

"Jesse, this is Lydia."

"Are you okay? Where are you?"

She gave him the address and told him which warehouse she was in. "I'm tying up Phillip Keats. Hurry. He has Kate somewhere. We have to make him tell us where."

"I'm not far away. I'm heading there now. Stay on the phone."

"First I'm putting it down to tie him up."

After she secured the bomber, she picked up the phone and stood. "This guy isn't going anywhere. He'll be out for a while. I'm searching for Kate."

"Wait. I'm pulling up behind the row of warehouses. Brutus is with me, and I have something from school with Kate's scent."

Lydia moved toward the opened door, went outside and waved at Jesse. "I'm so glad to see you."

Jesse parked, said something to Williams, then rushed toward her. He scooped her up in his arms and hugged her. "I love you. I can't lose you again."

"I love you, Jesse." She gave him a quick kiss. "That hasn't changed in all these years. But right now I have to find Kate. She's here because of me." She stepped away and saw Don bringing Brutus with Kate's backpack. Mary was behind them.

"We will find her and then we'll need to talk about why in the world you came to meet him alone and without letting us know."

"I left a message on my nightstand."

Jesse looked at Williams.

He shrugged. "I didn't see it, but the window was open and the wind was blowing into the room. It's probably on the floor by the bed or under it."

"I only told you the general location because that's all I knew, but I think he was following me so I had to come alone. Oh, and he had put a bug in Calvin's collar so he knew what was going on."

"How did you knock him out?" Mary asked as she examined the pharmacist while Don handed Jesse a flashlight.

"I gave him a tranquilizer. That's one of the perks of being a vet. I had some lying around my house."

Jesse held the backpack up for Brutus to smell. "Find." He gave his Rottweiler a long leash and he and Lydia followed. He yelled back to the officers, "Call this in and guard him."

Brutus headed for a rickety staircase and started up. Her heartbeat thundering in her head, Lydia held the light on the area in front of the dog. He entered a room, and she prayed Kate was alive and unharmed.

Jesse went in first and came to a stop. He called Brutus to his side. Lydia peered around Jesse to see her sister tied up with duct tape, some of it over her mouth. Her wide eyes, full of fear, were all Lydia could focus on.

Until Jesse said, "She has a bomb strapped to her."

FOURTEEN

Jesse handed Lydia the leash. "Leave with Brutus. I'll stay but everyone else needs to get out." He glanced at her. "No argument, Lydia. I have experience disarming bombs, but I can't be distracted with you being here. Go. Now."

"I can't leave you."

"Now. If there's a timer on it, I'm wasting valuable seconds."

Kate nodded as though indicating there was a timer. Lydia pulled Brutus toward her, took one last look at Jesse and Kate, then hurried down the stairs.

Jesse realized how much he had to live for. *Lord, we're in Your hands. Please keep us alive.*

Remembering how he triggered the bomb in the house, Jesse approached Kate sitting in a chair with duct tape securing her along with the bomb. He saw the timer. In red numbers, it indicated he had four minutes, twenty-three seconds to get her out of the chair and out of the building. Or to disarm it.

With his pulse racing, he squatted next to Kate and studied the bomb, similar to one he'd handled before. "We're going to be all right. I'm not letting anything happen to you. Lydia would never forgive me."

He dug into his pocket and removed his Swiss Army Knife. Then holding his breath, he cut the wire he thought would stop the timer. It did at two minutes, forty-one seconds.

After swiping the sweat from his brow, he removed the tape over Kate's mouth first.

Sirens blasted the air as Lydia stood at the end of the row of warehouses. She kept repeating her prayer to bring Jesse and Kate out alive.

Then she spied Jesse and Kate emerging from the building, and she raced toward them as the first responders arrived. Williams had called the bomb squad, and they were in the lead.

She threw her arms around Kate and held her tight. She pulled back, tears running down her face, the biggest smile on her face. "You are grounded for the rest of your life."

Her sister's eyes watered, and she hugged Lydia and sobbed. She stroked Kate's back, telling her she would be all right. Lydia's gaze connected with Jesse's, and she wanted to kiss him senseless.

On the drive home from visiting Connor at the hospital, Lydia looked at her sister while stopped at a red light. "We need to talk about what has been happening. You could have died."

"I'm so sorry, Lydia. I honestly didn't think anyone would be after me or watching me like that."

"How many times have you sneaked out of school?"

Kate lowered her head and twisted her hands together in her lap. "Four times." Her gaze reconnected with Lydia's. "But that was the first time we went to his

house. I wasn't going to let anything happen. I was…"
Tears glistened in her eyes. "He wanted to show me his
room. We were gonna be back at school by our next
class. That's only half an hour."

"As you can see a lot can happen in half an hour."

"He'd been so mad we hadn't spent any time alone
together in a while. I was trying to please…" Kate
sucked in a deep breath, tears streaking down her face.
"I was an idiot."

The light turned green, and Lydia crossed the inter-
section, not far from Jesse's house. "I hope you never
make the mistake I did. I paid dearly for it. I know sex
doesn't seem like a big deal to some, but there can be
big consequences."

Kate remained quiet for a few minutes, but when
Lydia pulled into Jesse's garage, her sister asked, "Can
I ask you a question?"

"Sure."

"Do you think you lost your daughter because of
what you did?"

"I can't answer that. She contracted a virus and died
in my womb. That can happen to anyone. I do know
that I lost Jesse because of what I did. I loved him—
still do—but I did the 'right' thing and married Aaron.
That was such a mistake, and for a long time I was mad
at God. But I've come to realize in this last year I'm a
stronger person, and my faith is deeper now because
of what I went through."

"Did Mom leave because of me?"

Lydia twisted toward her and took her hands. "No.
She left because of her. She didn't want her life. It really had nothing to do with us. It's taken me a long

time to realize that, too. We were abandoned, but our father did the best he could."

Kate's eyes grew round. "You can say that even after what he did to you?"

"Yes. I know he forgave me when he left me his practice and guardianship of you. Our dad was never a man of many words. He kept things inside." *So much like Jesse.* "But that action spoke volumes to me."

"Even though I've been a pain."

Lydia pulled her sister to her and hugged her. "You are my sister. I love you."

After a long afternoon and evening wrapping up the case, Jesse was glad to be home and to see Lydia. She'd wondered why Keats had gone to such lengths to cover up his mistress's death, and right before he left the station, Thomas had discovered Keats had a major gambling debt. He was using his wife's inheritance as a way to buy him some time with the collectors.

Jesse came into the kitchen from the garage and saw the two pieces of luggage sitting near the door. He could have lost Lydia today forever. He had no intentions of letting her go again.

He strolled into his living room. Lydia and Kate sat side by side on the couch, talking, smiling. Lydia glanced at him and whispered something to her sister.

Kate chuckled. "I'll be out back with Calvin, Mitch and Brutus. I want to say goodbye to them."

After she left, Jesse took her place on the couch. "Okay, what did you say to her?"

"We had a long talk together. I think we finally understand each other."

"No, I mean just now."

"I told her I was going to make sure you understand how important you are in my life."

One of his eyebrows lifted. "Oh, you are. Just how important am I?"

"This much." She held her arms out as far as she could. "I love you—always have, and I'm going to prove it to you."

His fingers delved into her hair, and he held her head still. "You don't have to prove a thing. I know you love me. I love you—always have."

His lips touched hers softly at first, then settled over her mouth as the kiss lengthened. He wrapped his arms around her and pressed her against him.

When he leaned back slightly, he gazed at her for a long moment. "I've always been so afraid to lose someone else important to me that I shut myself off from others. I promise not to, and if I do, let me know. I won't change overnight, but I want you to be with me for all the changes. Will you marry me?"

She cupped his face. "I've been waiting for those words for years. Yes. And soon."

He kissed her long and hard. "As soon as we can. I'm not waiting any longer." He'd finally found the family he'd been searching for.

* * * * *

Dear Reader,

The Protector's Mission is the third book in my Alaskan Search and Rescue series. In this story, Jesse Hunt is a K-9 police officer who gets caught up with a serial bomber. When he isn't doing his police work, he is volunteering for search and rescue operations in the Anchorage area. K-9 teams go above and beyond to find people. The dogs are amazing. I thought Alaska was the perfect setting for a series centered on search and rescue missions.

I love hearing from readers. You can contact me at margaretdaley@gmail.com or at PO Box 2074, Tulsa, OK 74101. You can also learn more about my books at www.margaretdaley.com. I have a newsletter that you can sign up for on my website.

Best wishes,

Margaret Daley

COMING NEXT MONTH FROM
Love Inspired® Suspense

Available October 6, 2015

LISCNM0915

REQUEST YOUR FREE BOOKS!

2 FREE RIVETING INSPIRATIONAL NOVELS
PLUS 2 FREE MYSTERY GIFTS

Love Inspired®
SUSPENSE
RIVETING INSPIRATIONAL ROMANCE

YES! Please send me 2 FREE Love Inspired® Suspense novels and my 2 FREE mystery gifts (gifts are worth about $10). After receiving them, if I don't wish to receive any more books, I can return the shipping statement marked "cancel." If I don't cancel, I will receive 4 brand-new novels every month and be billed just $4.99 per book in the U.S. or $5.49 per book in Canada. That's a savings of at least 17% off the cover price. It's quite a bargain! Shipping and handling is just 50¢ per book in the U.S. and 75¢ per book in Canada.* I understand that accepting the 2 free books and gifts places me under no obligation to buy anything. I can always return a shipment and cancel at any time. Even if I never buy another book, the two free books and gifts are mine to keep forever.

123/323 IDN GH5Z

Name	(PLEASE PRINT)

Address	Apt. #

City	State/Prov.	Zip/Postal Code

Signature (if under 18, a parent or guardian must sign)

Mail to the **Reader Service:**
IN U.S.A.: P.O. Box 1867, Buffalo, NY 14240-1867
IN CANADA: P.O. Box 609, Fort Erie, Ontario L2A 5X3

Are you a current subscriber to Love Inspired® Suspense books
and want to receive the larger-print edition?
Call 1-800-873-8635 or visit www.ReaderService.com.

* Terms and prices subject to change without notice. Prices do not include applicable taxes. Sales tax applicable in N.Y. Canadian residents will be charged applicable taxes. Offer not valid in Quebec. This offer is limited to one order per household. Not valid for current subscribers to Love Inspired Suspense books. All orders subject to credit approval. Credit or debit balances in a customer's account(s) may be offset by any other outstanding balance owed by or to the customer. Please allow 4 to 6 weeks for delivery. Offer available while quantities last.

LIS15

*Will a young Amish widow's life change when her
brother-in-law arrives unexpectedly at her farm?*

Read on for a sneak preview of
THE AMISH MOTHER
The second book in the brand-new trilogy
LANCASTER COURTSHIPS

"You're living here with the children," Zack said. *"Alone?"*

"This is our home." Lizzie faced him, a petite woman
whose auburn hair suddenly appeared as if streaked with
various shades of reds under the autumn sun. Her vivid
green eyes and young, innocent face made her seem
vulnerable, but she must be a strong woman if she could
manage all seven of his nieces and nephews—and stand
defiantly before him as she was now without backing
down. He felt a glimmer of admiration for her.

"*Koom.* We're about to have our midday meal. Join us.
You must have come a long way." She bit her lip as she
briefly met his gaze.

Zack still couldn't believe that Abraham was dead. His
older brother had been only thirty-five years old. "What
happened to my *brooder*?"

Lizzie went pale. "He fell," she said in a choked voice,
"from the barn loft." He saw her hands clutch at the hem
of her apron. "He broke his neck and died instantly."

Zack felt shaken by the mental image. "I'm sorry. I
know it's hard." He, too, felt the loss. It hurt to realize that
he'd never see Abraham again.

"He was a *goot* man." She didn't look at him when she bent to pick up her basket, then straightened. "Are you coming in?" she asked as she finally met his gaze.

He nodded and then followed her as she started toward the house. He was surprised to see her uneven gait as she walked ahead of him, as if she'd injured her leg and limped because of the pain. "Lizzie, are *ya* hurt?" he asked compassionately.

She halted, then faced him with her chin tilted high, her eyes less than warm. "I'm not hurt," she said crisply. "I'm a cripple." And with that, she turned away and continued toward the house, leaving him to follow her.

Zack studied her back with mixed feelings. Concern. Worry. Uneasiness. He frowned as he watched her struggle to open the door. He stopped himself from helping, sensing that she wouldn't be pleased. Could a crippled, young nineteen-year-old woman raise a passel of *kinner* alone?

Don't miss
THE AMISH MOTHER *by Rebecca Kertz,*
available October 2015 wherever
Love Inspired® books and ebooks are sold.

LIEXP0915R